Ada

Legend of a Healer

By
R. A. McDonald

House of Lore Publishing

www.HouseofLore.net

First House of Lore paperback edition, 2011

Summary: When Fifteen-year-old Ada finds out she has the power to heal, she sets out to solve the mystery surrounding the disappearance of her mother and learns that her true power is her will to survive. [1.Healing-Fiction.2.Mystery-Fiction. 3.Suspense-Fiction4.Romance-Fiction.5.Philosophical-fiction.]

ISBN 978-0-615-41258-0

Library of Congress Control Number: 2010915413

Printed and bound by
Edwards Brothers Inc., Ann Arbor, Michigan

Illustrations by James McDonald

To the sweetest snapdragons, without you two, our ship would be aimlessly adrift.

Grandmissy, you have always been the light in my dark sky. Thank you for easing my struggle.

Scrubtree, thank you for always believing. Your faith in me is my anchor.

Donald Sue, the caterpillar, your guidance has pulled me through many tight spots. Thank you.

Dr. M, thank you for lifting the blindfold from my eyes.

To a Master Artist and his wife wrapped in blue, your kindness is external warmth in what is seemingly a cold world.

To the possibilities we all have within us.

To the reader,
the power is within you!

"A cutting word is worse than a bowstring; a cut may heal, but the cut of the tongue does not."

--African Proverb

"We are healed from suffering only by experiencing it to the full."

--Marcel Proust

"The art of healing comes from nature, not from the physician. Therefore the physician must start from nature, with an open mind."

--Philipus Aureolus Paracelsus

"If you do a good job for others, you heal yourself at the same time, because a dose of joy is a spiritual cure."

--Dietrich Bonhoeffer

"How does one become a butterfly?" she asked pensively. "You must want to fly so much you are willing to give up being a caterpillar."

--From Hope For The Flowers

"To be yourself in a world that is constantly trying to make you something else is the greatest accomplishment."

--Ralph Waldo Emerson

"It is not the strongest of the species that survives, nor the most intelligent that survives. It is the one that is the most adaptable to change."

--Charles Darwin

1

Usually an indoor plant will bend and twist to find the direction with the most sun, but not the plant in Ada's room. All of its leaves were turned toward her bed which was in the darkest corner, and the place she spent most of her free time listening to music.

When she first came to live with her foster parents, Dave and Carla, the plant was almost dead with sagging branches and shriveled leaves. Ada poured a cup of water into the soil and watched it greedily absorb the liquid. If people were more like plants, quiet and simple, then none of this would have happened she thought touching the fleshy leaves.

Ada was happy about leaving. She'd been preparing for it the last couple of months. Carla stood in the open doorway watching to make sure she didn't steal anything. There wasn't much to take except a single bed and a small dresser. Ada smiled at the thought of pretending to pull the bed toward the door, but her smile quickly faded when she saw Carla's suspicious glare.

Pushing Carla any further wasn't an option. She just might make good on all of the threats of beating her grateful.

Unlike the last foster home, Ada had really tried to make an effort with Dave and Carla, but by the end of the first month it was war. Carla with her boxes of wine and evenings in front of the TV, and Dave always walking in on Ada while she was in the bathroom, and then apologizing as he groped her with his eyes; it was destined for failure. She zipped her canvas bag and sat her backpack on top of it.

"Carla!" Dave yelled from the kitchen. "Come here."

"You stay right in this room," she snarled.

Ada waited until the foot steps were gone and then opened the window and lowered the plant carefully to the ground. At least it would have a chance. Outdoors in Seattle, it was certain not to dehydrate. She grabbed her things and went to wait for Gretchen on the front porch. Gretchen was, for as long as Ada could remember, her disgruntled social worker.

Ada stopped in the living room to take in her artwork. In velvety black paint, on the biggest wall in the living room, Ada had drawn an enormous skull and crossbones encircled by all of the words Carla regularly screamed at her. She smiled noticing the streaks of deep red that surfaced in the black. It wasn't easy getting the red to show up, and she was glad she wasn't going to be around when Carla found the pasta pan she had used to mix the paint in. At around three in the morning, after her drunken stupor, Carla woke up and discovered Ada's project.

WORTHLESS
UNGRATEFUL
FREAK

Despite the time, she called Gretchen and demanded that she pick Ada up immediately.

Gretchen was always complaining of her workload being enough for two, so she came at her own pace, but always showed up. Ada had barely been sitting on the front step five minutes when Gretchen's silver sedan pulled in. As she reached down to grab her bags the screen door opened behind her. She turned around to see Dave and Carla standing in the doorway.

Ada paused and then looked directly at Dave."You should have your lungs checked."

"Get out!" they both yelled.

"Freak." Dave grumbled under his breath.

She walked away with a sense of satisfaction knowing that eventually, probably when it was too late, they would think of her again. She settled into Gretchen's car ready for the "burned all bridges" lecture. Ada always had one headphone plugged into her ear.

"I don't get it Ada, you're a pretty girl, intelligent and people generally like you, when they first meet you that is, but instead you dress like you don't care, you do stupid things to get yourself kicked out of school or your home, and you say the damndest things that just piss people off."

She pulled the car to the side of the road and turned toward Ada. "This is serious business this time."

Ada was looking at her black T-shirt and jeans wondering how they could be construed as not caring.

"How can you hear with this always crammed in your ear?" Gretchen yanked the headphone out.

"The background music makes crappy conversations like this bearable," Ada said putting the headphone back in.

Too bad her left headphone was blown, otherwise she would have completely blocked out Gretchen.

"You're fifteen-years-old now, not a cute little kid anymore. Unless we can get ahold of your aunt, they are going to send you straight to juvenile hall. Not even the group home this time."

She waved her hand in front of Ada who was staring in a daze out the window. "Hello!"

It had started to drizzle and drops of water were gathering then unraveling into tiny streams down the glass.

"You're hopeless!"

2

The Between House was smack in the middle of downtown Seattle. It got its name for being the place where foster kids sit in limbo while the state decides their fate. Ada sat on top of the stone wall that separated the Between House from the rest of the world so she could watch people without being noticed, her favorite form of socialization.

Gretchen was desperately pounding numbers into her cell phone trying to find someone who could open the doors. Apparently at the moment, Ada was the only kid caught between. The rain had stopped, but her breath still came out in white puffs. She leaned from side to side trying to keep her butt warm against the cold stone. A sea of people flowed down the street not noticing her perch. They all seemed so serious about their destinations. Everyone brushed past each other acting as if they were on an empty sidewalk.

A shiny, colorfully painted pig in front of a busy coffee shop caught her eye. It was five times the size of a real pig and had a slot in its back like a piggy bank. People were waiting in line to get their coffee and using it as a place to lean and talk.

All the while Gretchen's voice whined behind her, talking nonstop into her cell phone. The jail was soon to be opened. Ada turned back around to locate the fancy pig again. A fat, well dressed, old woman was posing for a picture in front of the pig, swallowing up the colorful middle with her own rotund belly, while a homeless man slowly felt his way along the backside looking for the slot to drop coins in. Ada couldn't help but laugh at the woman's fancy dress shoes intermingling with the peach painted hooves. The homeless man managed to bump the back of the woman and an argument started.

"You can get down from there now. Jared'll be here any second," Gretchen said annoyed, flipping her phone closed and tucking it in her purse.

When Ada turned back around to see what was happening with the argument she was disappointed to find the coffee shop owner shooing away the homeless man to the delight of the fat woman.

"Ada, come on," Gretchen called as Jared rattled keys trying to open the door. She thought about jumping down to the sidewalk and disappearing into the crowd, but she knew she'd only be exchanging one jail for another. She decided to go with the one that had a bed.

The Between House was small with few comforts. Ada passed through the kitchen. It was the most furnished room in the whole downstairs. A small fold out table with four matching chairs adorned the kitchen and dining room, and one roll top desk sat against an empty wall in the living room. She went straight upstairs to the room marked for girls and tossed her duffle bag on one of the six single beds lined up along the wall. Her backpack always stayed with her. If she wasn't wearing it, it was next to her. It held her important things, like her mini laptop and iPod.

Every birthday her aunt, the one Gretchen was frantically trying to contact, sent her a gift. Usually it was money or clothes but on her thirteenth birthday she received a book sized laptop and an iPod with a torn paper taped on it that read:

"Happy Thirteenth! Love, Aunt Jessie."

The only way to contact her aunt was through a post office box. Ada stopped sending thank you letters after her seventh birthday. There was never a reply, so she imagined her unopened letters were gathering dust in a stuffy post office. She had searched for her on the internet, but it was as if Aunt Jessie didn't exist. She lay on the bed closest to the window and stared at the clean fresh paint spots where someone had painted over words left behind by previous occupants. The contrast of yellow spongy stains on the ceiling made the room look like it belonged in a haunted house.

Ada turned her music louder to help block out Gretchen's heels tip tapping across the wood floors. Besides the beds, the only other piece of furniture was a mirrored medicine cabinet that hung on the wall. Clothes were supposed to stay in suitcases.

She leaned forward and gave the cord on the blind a hard tug causing it to wrap repeatedly around itself. The sky was hidden under a heavy blanket of clouds suffocating the city underneath and casting a grey shadow on everything.

She sat up and ran her finger along the window pane. It was painted shut. There was no way she was going back to a group home or to reform school. If it came down to it, she might try going it alone on the street, but so far Gretchen had managed to come through in the last minute with foster parents. Dealing with one or two adults was easier than being trapped with other kids. She unlocked the window and tried to open it but it didn't budge. The tip tap sound of Gretchen coming upstairs put her back to staring at the ceiling.

"Ada, you might as well get as comfortable as you can. You're going to be here for a couple of days," Gretchen said as she entered the room. "Don't worry about unpacking your things though."

"Oops, I already put everything away in the medicine cabinet," Ada said mockingly.

"You know, you're your biggest enemy. You've had plenty of opportunities at a good stable life," Gretchen said.

"Here's what I think of a good life," Ada said turning her head toward Gretchen. "Half of it's spent asleep, then when I'm awake, I get to watch the sickness and suffering of people that I could give a crap about.

Oh, and don't forget the assholes. Good luck avoiding them. Where's the time for a good life?" She went back to staring at the ceiling again, but could feel Gretchen watching her from the doorway. "Everyone hangs on for a stale crumb of the *good life*. It's all overrated." Ada said turning her back to Gretchen, and looking out the drizzly window.

"If I didn't know you so well, I'd put you on suicide watch." Gretchen tossed her a small bag of toiletries. "Hang in there Ada, you never know, you may get a taste of that prized happiness."

Ada waited for the faint tap of Gretchen's shoes to ensure she was alone and then searched her backpack for something sharp to break the paint lock around the window, just in case they did try to put her away.

By the second day Ada was sure she was being held captive. She wasn't allowed to go out to the courtyard or sit on the stone wall without supervision. The doors and windows were all locked.

"Trapping me like this has to be breaking fire codes," she grumbled, sitting down on the closet floor in her room to admire the countless signatures carved or written on the wall. She counted her name seven times and decided to make it eight when Gretchen knocked on the closet door.

"You in there Ada?"

Ada slid the small flashlight she had taken from Carla's glove box into her sweatshirt pocket. She opened the door and shut it behind her taking a seat on the bed as if she had just come out of another room instead of an empty cubbyhole.

"It looks like you're going to be here a bit longer than expected," Gretchen said with a somber look. She smoothed pretend wrinkles from her stiffly starched skirt. "To be honest, our choices are slim. Your aunt needs to call." Gretchen laid a tablet of paper and a pencil on the nightstand, "it might be a good idea to write an apology letter to Dave and Carla."

"Here, hand me a piece of that paper and I'll wipe my ass with it. You can send them that," Ada said flicking the pad and pencil off of the nightstand to the ground. "And Reform School! It's not like I committed a crime. It was self-defense." She stood and paced in front of the window.

"Vandalizing the inside of your foster parent's house is a big enough crime, especially with your record," Gretchen said snatching the pad of paper from the floor. "In past homes you were violent, disrespectful, you've stolen...

"Stolen! Only getting back because I was stolen from!"

"Listen Ada, I'm trying to look into other avenues, but we've exhausted pretty much all of them, and believe it or not I have people that I have to answer to, and they don't want to deal with you. They think you're trouble." She sat down on the edge of the bed again. "I've written another letter to your aunt telling her of your dire circumstances. She's really our last chance."

"You mean *my* last chance, which really means no chance at all." Ada stopped in front of the window. People survive living on the streets everyday she thought to herself as a car drove through a puddle splashing water onto the sidewalk.

"I'm sorry, but for the remainder of your time here, you're going to continue to be on lock-down."

Ada rested her head on the window wondering if she was that easy to read, "It's not like I didn't call and tell you about the crappy people you stuck me with. I even told you about freaky pervert Dave."

"You can't fight the system Ada. You need to learn to work with it."

"How does it feel being the world's shittiest social worker?" Ada said listening to the movement of Gretchen standing to leave.

"We only have three days max," she said going out the door and ignoring Ada's comment. "Your aunt better call."

"*I* only have three days, Gretchen!" Ada yelled after her as she listened to the fading sound of high heel shoes.

Better lose those shoes they're messing up your lower back Ada thought to herself as she went to the window. The paint was barely chipped after digging at it with a pen for almost an hour. She tossed the pen on the bed and stared out the window. There had to be another way to escape. The president was more likely to answer Gretchen's letter than Aunt Jessie.

Ada's third day in the Between House was busy with planning an escape. The front door was impossible; it was barred up like a jail cell, but people used the back door several times a day, at least twice for a shift change, and once for food. Two adults were always on shift. This allowed one of them to take a break or sleep while the other kept an eye on things. Her plan was to get a chance at the door when someone was coming in or out, so she could slip a wet wad of toilet paper in the hole where the lock latched. Getting to the door without drawing suspicion was going to be the hard part. It would require socializing which was what Ada dreaded most. Too many screw ups would draw attention, so timing was everything. Food was only allowed in the kitchen, so the opportunity for small talk was fairly easy while keeping an eye on the door.

Ada pressed her forehead against the window trying to see the street below. The night outside made the glass a shiny black wall. It was drizzling and the only thing visible was the shadowy area under a street light. From the outside, her lit up window would look like a TV screen to those interested in watching. She pulled the blind down and went to lean in the doorway of the room.

Gretchen was long gone, replaced by Erin and Jared. It was always the same: two college students completing field work studies by volunteering to work with troubled kids. Ada heard the clanging sound of dishes. She tiptoed down the stairs and saw Erin at the sink.

"Here let me help," Ada said grabbing a towel.

"Thanks. We haven't formally met yet." Erin held out a soapy hand.

"Let me guess, last year of college?"

"Yeah actually, this is my second week on call for this place," she said loudly over Ada's obnoxious clanging. "And you're the first person that I've had to come in for." She laid the dishrag neatly over the faucet and turned to Ada. "I know this isn't your first time here, but I'm sure they'll connect you with a good family."

"Weirder things have happened," Ada said tossing her towel on the counter and leaning against the cabinet to have a better look at Erin. "Have you ever had your airway checked?"

"Excuse me?" she said stepping back. "My what?"

"Your breathing passage. I don't know the scientific term," Ada said rubbing her throat. It never failed, people always reacted defensively. She looked toward the stairs thinking of going back to the room. People were never happy about having their health problems pointed out. That was one of the reasons she stayed away. It was easier to ignore a weird smell or an annoying rattle at a distance. The worst was when she could feel it, like walking into a room after an argument, nobody's saying anything, but the tension's there. With Erin, it was a continuous rattling accompanied by a whisper of a wheeze.

"Sorry, just forget it," Ada said heading for the stairs.

"Wait a minute," Erin took a seat at the table. "Did you come down to help or play head games?"

Ada ignored her and went back to the room and lay on the bed listening to music. Within a few minutes Erin came and sat on the bed across from her. She waited patiently until Ada pulled the headphone from her ear.

"Why did you ask me about my airway?"

"I shouldn't have. I'm not in here for the eighth time because I'm normal. Please, just forget it." She rolled over and faced the covered window hoping Erin would take the hint, but the bed sank at her feet.

"I was just diagnosed with asthma, but nothing they've given me has helped."

"It's not Asthma," Ada said without hesitation propping herself up against the headboard.

"This is my health we're talking about. This is ridiculous, how would you know? "

"If I can hear it; you have to be able to feel it," Ada said watching Erin feel her throat and chest. "Maybe something's caught in there."

"I don't remember choking on anything," Erin mumbled to herself.

"Well then, it's Asthma," Ada said abruptly turning back toward the window. She lay there hardly breathing until she felt Erin's weight lift from the bottom of the bed.

"By the way," Erin said from across the room. "Gretchen will be here bright and early tomorrow. Jared says she has some news for you." She turned the light out as she left. Ada didn't move until the sound of footsteps disappeared downstairs.

"It can't be this quick," she said jumping out of bed and flipping on the light. She grabbed her duffle bag and sat it by the door. If she didn't get out before Gretchen came, there was no getting out.

It was four in the morning when the house was finally silent, so Ada got out of bed carefully trying to minimize creaking. There wasn't time to jam the lock. She had thought up an alternative plan while waiting for Erin and Jared to go to sleep. With such short notice there were few options. Finding a hiding place was the safest and quickest solution. She could stay hidden until they left to look for her. Once she was alone, she would find a way out even if it meant breaking a window, but she had to find the perfect hiding spot. She thought of the attic, with its door in the hallway ceiling that pulled down and folded out into stairs, but it would be too noisy to open let alone climb up. There was only one other place she could think of that had an area that tucked back out of sight, the cupboard under the kitchen sink. It was close to the back door and stretched deep under the counter.

The rumbling engine of a street cleaner slightly rattled the window. It was now or never. She tied her hair into a ponytail expecting the cupboard to be dark and dusty. She grabbed her bags slipping the flashlight into her pocket.

Ada made her way downstairs staying close to the wall. The silence was thick like cotton in her ears. She didn't turn her flashlight on until she was well in the doorway of the kitchen. Daybreak offered just enough light to avoid bumping into walls. When she opened the cupboard it made a tiny creak that seemed to echo through the silent house. She held her breath and listened. No one moved upstairs so she continued.

The cupboard was empty except for dish soap and a sponge. She moved them to the side and poked her head in. A moist mildew smell filled her nose reminding her of a cellar. She crawled partially in to have a better look and flicked on her flashlight. Someone would have to crawl halfway in to see her. It would be tight squeezing past the tangle of rusty plumbing. There was about two feet of space that tucked back to the left side. Barely enough room to wedge her duffle bag in. Her flashlight caught dangling silky strands of dusty spider webs hanging from the corners. She slammed her head on the top of the cabinet as she pulled back and shook her hair for spiders.

Both bags were stacked in the back corner when she heard someone stirring upstairs. She gave another violent shake at the thought of spiders, pulled her hood up and squeezed in. Her heart pounded when she couldn't close the cupboard doors completely. Using her fingernail against a thin ridge she pulled them shut. She brought her knees close and leaned forward making sure only her butt and feet had to touch anything. Her eyes were wide open but the blackness swallowed everything. Constant tickling feelings caused her to whack her elbow on a pipe, rattling the sink. She covered her face with her hands and waited. Between the mildew smell, which was now a nauseating taste, and the feeling of spiders crawling in her clothes she was ready to give up and go back to her room when she heard slamming doors and raised voices.

"I checked the bathroom."

"She's not here either." A thin light suddenly seeped into the cupboard. She could hear doors opening and closing along with frantic footsteps.

"Her stuff's gone too. Shit, I've never lost a kid before." Jared's voice boomed from outside the cupboard.

"We didn't lose her. I'm sure she somehow ran away." The shadow of legs blocked part of the light at the bottom of the cupboard doors. A loud boom caused Ada to jump and knock the wall behind her. She covered her mouth waiting to see if they heard.

"Relax Jared, we'll find her."

"It's almost seven. Gretchen's going to be here any minute," he grumbled. "Did you tell the kid she has news?"

"Yeah, I told her."

Ada heard a light knock and then a door opened and closed.

"I'd like to know how she got out." Gretchen's voice snapped followed by the sharp clicking of her high heels.

"She ran away," Jared blurted.

"Excuse me?" asked Gretchen's annoyed voice.

Ada couldn't help but smile.

"Her stuff's gone and she's gone." A kitchen chair screeched along the floor followed by the sound of someone sitting down with a loud thump.

Erin's voice broke the silence, "listen guys, I'm not trying to run out on you, but I have a doctor appointment in less than an hour. I'll be back as quick as I can." Keys rattled and then the back door opened and closed. Ada rested her chin on her knees.

"This is unbelievable, a fifteen-year-old. How did she get out?"

"I wish I knew," Jared mumbled.

"Well, did she break a window or pry a lock?"

"Nope, just gone without a trace."

"Oh, I see, you didn't read her file." Gretchen's shoes tapped past the cupboard. Ada felt her face flush with anger at the thought of a file holding the key to her character. She thought she heard a low whisper and held her breath to listen. Soft footsteps and an occasional door closing lightly were all she could make out. She snuggled back into the corner. Spiders were the least of her worries now.

"Okay, well I'm really in a spot here." Gretchen's voice sounded like it was echoing through the house. "After all my letters, I finally received a phone call from Jessie, Ada's aunt. She'll be so disappointed."

Ada pulled her knees closer. She knew tricking Gretchen wouldn't be easy. Was she telling the truth or was this just a ploy to get her to come out?

"I suppose I should call Jessie and tell her not to bother coming." The emotion and high pitch in Gretchen's voice let Ada know it was definitely an act. Ada sat up straight when she heard beeps of a cell phone dialing out. Was Gretchen actually calling to cancel with Aunt Jessie?

Ada flung the cupboard doors open and lunged out head first shaking her hair and brushing her shoulders for spiders.

"Did you really talk to her or was that just a lie to get me to come out?" she asked as she pulled her bags from under the sink.

"Actually it's true. She called last night inquiring about your situation." Gretchen smiled triumphantly glancing at a stunned Jared. "I explained all that happened and the options that are left. She intends to take over full guardianship of you tomorrow morning. It's just a matter of paperwork." Jared cleared his throat loudly. He stood in the doorway arms crossed and glared at Ada.

"How much longer is she going to be here?" he asked Gretchen.

"Tomorrow morning her aunt picks her up." She smiled at Ada.

"Too bad we can't handcuff her to something," Jared said disappearing into another room. Ada picked up her bags and started for the stairs wondering if she'd even recognize her aunt.

"Hey, this is the miracle we were hoping for, you know a little bit of the good life!" Gretchen yelled after her while answering her cell phone.

Ada tossed her bag against the wall and sat at the edge of the bed fishing her iPod out of her backpack. She quickly lay back against the bed when she heard Gretchen tapping up the stairs.

"If you want to talk I'm sitting in for Erin. She's having some kind of emergency procedure done and won't be back," Gretchen said from the doorway.

Ada nodded without taking her eyes off of the ceiling. She couldn't help but wonder why her aunt was showing up now. She was the one who had put Ada in foster care in the first place. Her file listed her mother as "disappeared without a trace." The few memories she had of childhood had to have been with her aunt, but she couldn't remember a face no matter how hard she tried. She pulled the cord on the window blind. The sun was reflecting off of the wet street making it look like shiny metal. Ten years later and all of a sudden Aunt Jessie decides to come to the rescue, there has to be a catch she thought.

Ada's eyes opened at six in the morning. Tossing and turning all night made her feel like she hadn't slept at all. Aunt Jessie was supposed to arrive at eight, but unlike Gretchen most people that passed through Ada's life were chronically late, so she imagined she wouldn't meet her aunt until afternoon. She peeked out the door and was surprised to see Jared sitting on a chair with dark circles under his eyes reading a book. Hiding or sneaking out hadn't crossed her mind since she knew her aunt was coming. If she wanted to do that it would be much easier to leave with her aunt and then run away. The angry look on Jared's face made her keep her remarks to herself.

Gretchen kept the bathroom tied up for an hour. Ada liked to be quick about getting ready. Her hair was either hanging straight to her shoulders or back in a pony tail. She spent as little time as possible in the shower thanks to her last foster father. Wearing makeup wasn't an option. She couldn't afford it and she only liked to carry what she thought was absolutely necessary, two changes of clothes and one of anything else she needed. It was less tempting to those who like to steal or rifle through her stuff. She was pulling her hair back into a ponytail when the downstairs doorbell rang. She tiptoed to the top of the stairs to listen.

Gretchen's voice echoed upstairs, "you must be Jessie O'Neil. It's nice to finally meet you."

Ada went quickly back to her room. She checked the time on her watch. It was 7:45am, she's early.

Quietly, with both bags, she tiptoed downstairs and took a seat on the bottom step.

"You have no permanent address to list Mrs. O'Neil?" Gretchen asked pleadingly.

"It can be temporary, but just something that shows Ada will have a roof overhead."

"It's Ms. I've never been married," Jessie said softly. Ada had to strain to hear her. "I travel with my work. We'll be staying at hotels and occasionally with friends." Ada pictured a tall woman in an expensive suit.

"Can I at least list your company?"

"I work for myself, selling herbs and such." There goes the fancy suit, maybe khaki pants and a tee shirt.

There was a moment of silence that caused Ada to scoot to the edge of the stair and lean forward.

"What about school?" Gretchen asked.

"I'll be teaching her myself."

"You're the only family member we have listed. It would just make it a lot easier if we had some residence or contact number besides the P.O. Box." Gretchen pleaded.

There was another silence. Ada could feel her chance at freedom slipping away. She stood just in case she needed to bolt out the door if Aunt Jessie decided to give up and leave.

"I really want Ada to get this break. She's had it hard being shuffled from foster home to foster home," Gretchen said. Ada heard the rustle of papers.

"How about for the first year Ada contacts me

monthly to keep me up to date on how the traveling lifestyle is working for her?"

"Alright," Jessie answered without hesitation.

"So the first Tuesday of each month I'll expect a phone call." There was more paper shuffling. "If you would just sign here Ms. O'Neil to make it official."

"Am I buying a new car or taking my niece home."

Ada smiled thinking she may like her aunt after all.

"Well, I can see the relation," Gretchen said. "Let me get her, she should have already been down here."

"I'm here," Ada appeared from around the corner smiling. She was taken back at the sight of her aunt. She was a small woman with short, light brown hair that had grey patches at the temples. The only thing they had in common was the pale skin. She was dressed in jeans and a tee shirt with a colorful peace sign on the front. Her aunt also seemed taken back. She stared silently at Ada for a brief moment then held out her hand.

"Pays to stay close when people are discussing your future," she smiled warmly at Ada.

"You mean *deciding* my future." Ada shook the outstretched hand.

"You can call me Jessie. I hope that's everything." She nodded toward Ada's bags. "Let's get moving we have places to go and people to see," her aunt said energetically as she stood to leave.

"Don't forget Tuesday,"Gretchen said with an imploring smile as she handed both Ada and Jessie contact information.

3

Once out of the Between House, Ada had to half walk and run to keep up with Jessie.

"I'm not trying to lose you," Jessie said over her shoulder. "But we have a bus to catch and we can't be late."

In no time Ada was ushered onto a crowded Greyhound bus. Jessie pointed to a window seat and then went to speak to the driver. Ada put her duffle bag under the seat in front of her and rested her backpack against her leg. She stared out the window at a man loading luggage onto the bus.

"Have you been to Canada before?" Jessie asked as she sat down next to her. A head shake no was all the reply Ada felt like giving.

"Oh, it's a lovely country. Quite different from what you're used to."

"Why now after all this time?" Ada asked abruptly.

Jessie paused thoughtfully. "Honestly, because I'm always traveling with my work and a young girl needs stability. Foster care seemed like a safe choice. I didn't want you in a government institution."

"Institution! What am I insane?" Ada snapped.

"It's been hard for you, I know." Jessie reclined back as if going to sleep. "It was preparation for what's to come."

"What's that supposed to mean." Ada turned in her seat to face her aunt.

Jessie closed her eyes, "I need rest. We'll talk later I promise."

Despite Ada's squirming and an occasional clearing of her throat, Jessie slept almost the entire ride.

As quickly as they stepped off of the bus they were back to rushing from one place to the next. To Ada's disappointment there wasn't a moment to engage her aunt in conversation, but the new surroundings quickly caught her interest. Manicured plant life framed everything. Skyscrapers stood tall and slender giving the city an elegant and polished appearance. When Jessie stopped and bought a newspaper from a man in a corner grocery Ada noticed a subtle difference in the way he spoke. It didn't seem like a four hour bus trip could have taken her so far from what she was used to.

They went inside a bakery where Jessie bought a lunch, to go. On the way out the door she handed Ada the bag of food.

"You'll have a place to eat and a nice view in a few minutes."

Alone? Was Jessie leaving her somewhere, by herself, in a foreign country? Ada wondered slowing her pace and watching the back of Jessie get further away.

For several blocks she could smell the sweet decay of seaweed and feel the moisture of sea spray hanging behind the diesel and car exhaust. The business buildings soon faded to luxury hotels and apartment buildings. After several turns they faced the rolling waves of blue that stretched to the horizon. She followed Jessie onto a sandy beach speckled with a few oversized logs. The sun was out, but a cool wind swept off the water and made Ada thankful she had a sweatshirt. Her aunt stopped in front of a log. Its topside was polished flat by the numerous people that had used it as a seat.

"I'll be in there." Jessie nodded toward an old hotel almost completely consumed by ivy. Only the numerous windows and small glimpses of brick hinted at an actual building underneath.

"I'm meeting a friend about business," she mumbled avoiding Ada's suspicious gaze. She disappeared through a door at the bottom of the hotel.

Why all the secrecy? Ada wondered taking a seat on the log. As often as her aunt left her alone it wouldn't be hard to get away if things got too annoying. There was a turkey sandwich and a donut in the bag. She finished off the donut and began slowly picking away at the sandwich. A man and woman with three kids laid towels and beach bags near her log. Ada shivered watching as they stripped down to swimsuits and headed toward the bay's icy water. The angle of the log allowed her to keep an eye on the hotel and still watch what was going on in the water.

"Once you get in, it's not that bad." A boy that looked around her age said as he sat down next to her on the log.

She continued to eat her sandwich ignoring his attempt at conversation. He was tall with brown hair and blue eyes. His overly self-confident smile told her that he expected girls to happily respond.

"They say cold water is healthy," he continued, "but you don't have to worry about that."

Usually when she disregarded people they walked away; a few might even join in the silence, but this guy was already assuming her worries. She stuffed the remains of her sandwich into the paper bag while scouting for another log.

"So, are you just like your friend in there?" he nodded toward the hotel.

Surprised that he might know more about this visit than she did, she turned toward him. "How would I be like her?"

He smiled at her as if they both shared a secret. Normally people looked away when Ada gave them her hard look, but he soaked in her stare as though he thought she couldn't resist looking at him. She rolled her eyes and looked back toward the family who continued to happily torture themselves in the cold water. They finally made it to the floating dock with the tall metal slide, and were now climbing one after another to the top. She cringed at the thought of how cold the ocean wind and metal must feel against their wet skin.

"I figured you guys must be in the same line of work. I mean, I think it's great what she does for people."

"What do you mean by line of work?" she asked hoping for some information.

He looked at her with an expectant smile, "I know we're not supposed to talk about it, but my dad's grateful for all the favors."

Between his weird smile and talk of favors she was beginning to get uncomfortable.

"It's amazing the effect her visits have on people."

"Okay, I've heard enough." She looked at the hotel suspiciously. What kind of business was her aunt doing anyway? All the way to Canada for what, to meet some creepy guy at a hotel to do some favors.

"Just Great!" She stood up, grabbed her bags and headed toward the water.

"Hey, what's wrong? Where are you going?" He came up beside her with a confused look.

"Can you get away from me; I don't even know you," she said as she turned back toward the hotel.

"I'm sorry, your aunt has been helping my dad out for a long time. I just think it's cool."

"Listen," she said as she stopped and faced him, "I don't want to hear anymore about this freaky stuff. I am not like her. Now can you please leave me alone." She found another log to sit on that still had a view of the hotel.

Shortly after the boy left Jessie came out of the hotel followed by a man who quickly disappeared around the corner. She spotted Ada and motioned her over.

"It took longer than I expected." She turned toward the beach. "Let's walk. There's a park I want to show you."

Ada trailed behind Jessie until they stopped on a path in front of a large pond crowded with ducks. A man sat in a booth at the end of the trail selling seeds.

"Wait here," Jessie said as she headed toward the booth. Ada searched for a place to set her bag that wasn't covered with duck poop and feathers. A stubby branch on a small tree was her only option. The ducks seemed to have a built in sense when food was on its way. They poured out of the pond and crowded around Ada in anticipation of Jessie's return. Ada felt like joining her duffle bag and backpack in the tree, but Jessie arrived and took some of the attention.

"Here, they love it," she said handing Ada a paper bag bulging with seeds. Small beaks tugged at her jeans. She quickly threw handfuls of seeds to quiet the impatient honking. It was impossible to hold a conversation so she focused on emptying her bag. She felt a hard pinch on her butt and turned to find a large swan forcing its way to the food bag. She sprinkled the rest of the seeds on its head.

"I'm out of here," she yelled to Jessie grabbing her stuff and making a run for the street where she stopped and waited. Jessie followed laughing at the aggressive birds hissing and pecking.

"I already have a hotel room. It's this way."

"What kind of work do you do exactly?" Ada asked not budging.

"This isn't really the place to talk about that. I know this isn't easy for you but why don't we give it a chance. Here, let me carry that for a bit." She reached for Ada's duffel bag.

"That's alright, I got it." Ada followed Jessie back to an old motel in a shady neighborhood. The room was small with two single beds. There was a suitcase under a sink in the corner. Ada noticed a black wig laying on the counter near the sink. This just keeps getting weirder she thought to herself. The hotel didn't seem like a place that would have internet access, but it was worth a try. She pulled out her laptop and searched for a connection.

"I need to go to the office and let them know we'll be leaving tomorrow."

Ada nodded, wondering where they'd be headed next. The hotel didn't offer internet access, but she managed to connect to a non-secure line from across the street.

"Hey," she said before Jessie shut the door. "I never got a chance to say thanks for the laptop and iPod."

"I'm glad you enjoy them," Jessie said smiling as she closed the door.

Ada didn't like to judge people, especially her only known relative, but there were some things she just didn't want to be around and prostitution was one of them. She searched for information on Canadian prostitution laws.

"Just what I thought, it's legal," she said aloud.

"What's legal?" Jessie said closing the door behind her.

Ada closed her laptop and put it in her backpack.

"I really need to get back to Seattle," she said grabbing her things. "I appreciate the rescue and all but your line of work is not the life for me."

"Hold on," she gave Ada a puzzled look. "It would be a very long and dangerous walk back to the bus station right now." She paused, "I'm not exactly sure what you mean, but as for my line of work it's actually quite fulfilling."

"This doesn't have to get gross," Ada said moving toward the door.

"Not everyone has the gift Ada, but I think you might."

"You rescued me from juvenile hall to try and recruit me into prostitution? Well give it up because I'd rather be dead!" she yelled over Jessie's burst of laughter.

"What in the world made you think that I'm a prostitute?" she said dropping onto the bed. "I can assure you; I've made my share of mistakes, but prostitution is not one of them."

"What about that guy you met and his weird son?"

"Joseph's son said I was a prostitute?" Jessie interrupted.

"Pretty much, he said you and his dad had been doing business for a long time."

Ada flushed at her lack of proof.

"We have, but not that kind of business, believe me." She stood and rested her hand on Ada's shoulder. "I haven't been very forthcoming with information, but if you could trust me for the next few days, I promise everything will start to make sense. It won't be easy." She took Ada's bag and sat it next to hers. "But it will make sense."

Ada woke up the next morning to the thick mist and pattering sound of Jessie's shower. She felt a deep crease on her cheek from using her backpack as a pillow.

"There's still hot water. Not much pressure, but it gets the job done," Jessie said poking her head out of the bathroom. Ada took her typical three minute shower and five minutes to get ready to Jessie's surprise, and then sat on the bed listening to music.

"Do you remember much about your childhood?"

"Not really, only lots of animals."

Jessie smiled, "that was when I could stay somewhere long enough to have animals." She sat on the edge of the bed next to Ada.

"You look just like your mother, the same dark hair and milky, white skin. She was a beautiful woman."

"Are you really my aunt?" Ada asked pulling her headphone out. "I mean, we couldn't look any more different."

"You're quick like her too." She sat silently staring at the wall. "No, I'm not your aunt. Your mother and I were friends." She patted Ada on the knee, stood up and started packing again. "When you were a baby she asked me to take care of you and then she just disappeared."

"Where?"

"Simone is a strong willed woman. I tried to contact her every way I knew how." Jessie stopped talking and occupied herself with packing.

Ada had only seen her mother's name in her file; no one had ever said it aloud, and there were no pictures. She slid to the edge of the bed watching Jessie fumble with her bag.

"What about my dad? Did he look for her?"

"I never knew who he was and your mother never spoke of him." Jessie sat her bag in front of the door. "We should get going. I have business to take care of."

Ada prodded with more questions about her mother, but Jessie either didn't know or didn't want to talk about it.

They walked into the front office of the motel to return the key. The front wall, including the door, was entirely glass. Ada found a brochure stand to browse through. It was packed with more sightseeing than anyone could hope to do. She pulled out a pamphlet advertising a museum filled with wax representations of people, some still alive others long dead. "Weird," she said sliding it back in its pouch. A picture of a long foot bridge made of thick wire that stretched across a deep ravine caught her eye.

"Now this would be cool," she said to herself.

"You think?" Jessie asked looking over her shoulder. "It's in a beautiful park. I'm sure the views are stunning. Hold on to that. If we have time we'll go there. Better yet, we'll make time." Jessie grabbed a brochure of the bridge and slid it into a small pocket on her suitcase.

Ada ate her breakfast while trying to keep up with Jessie. They finally stopped in front of a small hospital. Joseph, the man Ada saw at the beach coming out of the ivy covered hotel, was waiting for them. It was still early morning so the air was crisp and damp. A layer of dew clung to everything giving off a fairy tale shine. She could hear chatter but there wasn't a bird in sight. She crumbled the rest of her bagel and threw it on the lawn stopping to see if they would take the bait.

"This way Ada." Jessie directed her around to the back of the hospital where Joseph held an emergency exit door open for them. It was Ada's first visit to any type of hospital and the smell was unbearable. Cleaning chemicals and medicine were overpowered by the smell of sickness. She stayed by the door and watched Jessie walk deeper into the sterile white hallway. Feeling the door lever against her back she decided to make a quick escape. As she leaned back against it an alarm ripped through the silent hallway. All she could do was stare at the screaming door in dismay wishing she could rip it from its hinges. Jessie and Joseph raced back to her.

"Are you alright?"

"We came through the back to avoid attention,"

Joseph growled as he shoved a circular key into a hole on the lever stopping the ruckus.

"I can't go in here. It reeks," Ada said eyeing the exit.

Jessie smiled resting her hand on Ada's shoulder. "Bear with me. We won't be here long."

Ada caught Joseph's annoyed glance and matched it with a hard stare.

"Fine. Whatever." Breathing through her mouth offered little help as Jessie guided her down the hall.

Every door they passed held the dread of seeing a dead person slumped over waiting to be rushed away to an area with even less color and sound. They stopped in front of oversized double doors that led to an extension of the maze they had just walked through.

"Wait here for me, I won't be long." Jessie pointed to a small, empty waiting room. Ada sat down reluctantly and watched the doors close. The waiting room consisted of three chairs, some outdated magazines, and a window that looked out to a small yard. It wasn't long before counting the endless amount of hairline cracks on the white wall became a bore. Music helped, but she was curious to know what was going on behind the doors and no one was around to question. Everything seemed so secretive. What kind of business brings people in the back door of a hospital, organ theft or worse stealing dead bodies? It was time to find out.

Ada quietly opened one of the doors just enough

to fit her head through. There was the same long, white hallway this time with several people, some in wheelchairs, waiting around a closed door. Is Jessie inside that room? Ada wondered. A large hand grasped her shoulder yanking her from the doorway. She stood face to face with a woman the size of an amazon. Her nurse's uniform fit like an adult wearing a child's coat.

"Why are you sneaking around here?" Her gruff voice matched the broad cut of her jaw line. She kept a tight grip on Ada's shoulder. The jeans and tennis shoes confirmed that she wasn't a nurse.

"Terry, you there?" a voice echoed from a two-way radio clipped to her belt.

"Yeah, Something's going on over here. Better come check it out." As she hooked the radio back in her belt Ada wrenched her shoulder free.

"Get back here." She lunged at Ada who quickly slid a chair between them.

"I just want to ask you a couple of questions."

Ada knew her only chance was to get through the double doors, but the amazon seemed to recognize her need. She maneuvered her around the room like a soccer ball, keeping her away from the doors in the process. Ada saw her chance when the amazon stumbled over an upside down chair. She juked past and yanked open one of the doors landing in Joseph's arms.

"What the hell!" Two men stood behind him dressed in legitimate hospital uniforms. The amazon burst through the door and stumbled to a stop. Joseph quickly shoved Ada behind him.

"This area of the hospital is closed." He noticed the makeshift uniform and stepped forward backing Terry out of the hallway. Ada watched as the two men escorted her away. Joseph came back and knocked on the door where the people were gathered. Jessie stepped out closing the door behind her.

"They know you're here," Joseph said.

"That was quick." She shook her head and walked over to Ada. "Are you alright?"

"If being chased by a freaky giant woman is considered alright." She wanted to ask what was going on but the serious look on both of their faces made her wait. Joseph brought in their bags.

"We're going to figure out who's leaking information, believe me. Just give me a couple more days."

"You know where we'll be," Jessie said motioning Ada to follow.

They left a different way than they came. It seemed like four or five blocks of hospital corridors. Jessie was in a paranoid hurry, always looking over her shoulder and slowing down when they came to a corner as if someone would jump out. When Ada caught herself constantly looking back at the slightest noise she stopped and dropped her bag on the ground.

"I'm not going anywhere till I know what's going on."

Jessie rushed back. "Not now, I'll tell you when we get where we're going." She grabbed Ada's bag and kept glancing down the empty hallway they had just come from.

"Who's following us?"

Jessie set the bag back on the ground when she saw Ada's stubborn expression.

"See, this is why I left you in foster care, right under their noses. I didn't want you to have to spend your life on the run."

"Whose noses?" Ada asked getting nervous over the frightened look Jessie would make at the faintest sound. The halls were empty and lined with closed doors. They seemed to be in a janitorial area of the hospital.

"The senator and his hired help." Jessie picked up Ada's bag and handed it to her. "If they see you with me you'll never be free."

"I get it. You're one of those conspiracy freaks." Ada said mockingly sliding down the wall to have a seat. "We all have microchips in our heads, so the government knows our every thought and move."

The sound of footsteps and a low rumble of voices brought her to her feet. Jessie had already found an open janitor's closet to slip into. The voices were just around the corner when she hurried Ada inside, closing the door behind them. Light slipped through where the bottom of the closet door didn't quite meet the floor. Ada got on all fours and laid her cheek on the cold, gritty cement. The fancy white tile stopped outside the closet.

Several shiny men's black dress shoes and a couple pairs of tennis shoes hurried past.

"This is stupid," she said standing up and brushing herself off. "We're in a hospital. People walk down halls all the time. What's weird is hiding in a stupid broom closet." She flung open the door and stepped out before Jessie could stop her. The corridor was empty in both directions.

Jessie let out a breath and leaned against the door frame.

"I know it's time I explained things to you. Let's just leave the hospital and we'll talk."

"Great, I hate this stinking place. I'd rather be sick than stay here."

"Have you ever been sick?" Jessie asked walking a few paces ahead. She turned into an empty hospital room; Ada quickly followed.

"Well, have you ever been sick?" She opened a window and dropped both bags outside. Large trees and a hedge blocked the view. She turned toward Ada waiting for her answer.

"I don't remember. Probably."

"That's what I thought. Indulge my paranoia one more time by using the window, and I'll explain what I can."

They left the hospital without a problem. Jessie steered her away from three parked cars that had fancy tinted windows, and forced her into a bush when a helicopter passed overhead.

After an hour of walking Jessie finally chose a café on a street blocked off from traffic. Ada was still removing thorns from her hair and clothes. Remnants of the bush she was shoved into.

Jessie said nothing until they were quietly seated in front of a window at the far corner of the café.

"What's wrong with him?" Jessie asked leaning in on the table.

"Who?" Ada said leaning back in her chair as far as she could without falling over.

"No more playing dumb. The man sitting at the coffee bar, his left lung is barely working because of a large growth. The woman that just left with the tray of coffee, blood infection, science calls it Hepatitis C. I saw your reaction at the hospital."

After a few moments of silence Ada leaned forward. "It's not the left lung, it's the right, but I'm sure you knew that."

"You're a bright girl Ada, stubborn and suspicious, but with good cause I'm sure."

"I would've actually believed you were my aunt if I knew you could see sickness too. Most people get really pissed if you say something is wrong with their health."

"I only want to help you." Jessie reached out toward Ada's hand but it quickly disappeared under the table. "It was necessary to hide you in order to still be able to help you."

"So, my mom could tell when people were sick too, that's why you guys were friends?" Ada asked leaning in closer.

"You have a pretty smile. I hope to see more of it." Jessie took a sip of tea, "Have you ever tried to heal the sickness you've recognized?"

Ada gave a puzzled expression making it obvious that the thought had never occurred to her.

"Heal. What are you talking about?" she whispered loudly. The woman behind the coffee bar looked up.

"I suppose you haven't had many opportunities to heal anyone," Jessie said.

"I've told a couple people they should go see a doctor, but that didn't go over well."

"Just think about it for a second. Have you ever been hurt and made it go away?" Jessie asked intently.

Ada stared silently remembering one of the few times she was hurt. The clatter of coffee cups faded to the sound of jump rope beads crashing against cement like a tap dancer keeping a beat. The circling arms of the girls blurred as they tried to out-do the girl in the middle jumping in place. She didn't see who lost grip of their end. It was a complete surprise when the handle lashed her open eye. A nearby teacher screamed and started toward her. All she could think of was the tearing pain as if her eyeball was split down the middle. She grabbed it with her hand and bent over pressing her face to her knees.

The teacher's arm slid across her shoulders, "It's going to be alright." Her voice came out in a breathless panic. "Let's have the nurse take a look." By the time they reached the nurse's office the pain was gone. When she moved her hand away only wet eyelashes identified the eye that had been hit. Several tests were performed at the request of the dismayed teacher, but there was no sign of injury.

Jessie's voice brought her back in focus, "you've got a lot to learn about yourself Ada, but there'll be enough time for that. There's a place I want to show you that I'm sure you're going to love."

She dropped a couple dollars on the table and was out the door as Ada scrambled to gather her senses and her things.

4

It was Ada's first time on a ferry. Seagulls swooped and screeched next to the boat dangerously close to the churning foam. The wind on deck whipped hair in every direction keeping Jessie inside. Ada spent the entire trip on deck thinking about what Jessie had said. Being able to heal explained some of the strange occurrences during her childhood. Getting immunization shots for school was always a traumatic event. It wasn't that the shots were painful. It was the alarmed reaction of the nurse when the injected fluid inevitably oozed back out of the injection site. A few nurses gave it another try, but the results were always the same.

Could she heal every injury? She wanted to know, but intentionally hurting herself was much more difficult than she'd imagined. She envied the little five-year-old who tripped onto the deck skinning her knee bloody. Jessie waved her inside as a voice called for passengers to get ready for arrival.

An hour ride in a taxi brought them to the mouth of a dirt road that disappeared into a labyrinth of green. Jessie wouldn't allow the taxi driver to take them any further.

"You'll appreciate it more if we walk," she said while Ada watched the tail lights fade into the distance.

"Try to imagine what it was like for an explorer who came upon this."

Ada rolled her eyes as Jessie started down the dirt road. The annoyingly long walk didn't detract from the view the road opened up to. Weather beaten trees framed a sandy boulder strewn cove. The ocean roared in bursts onto the rocky beach, much different than the beach with the silver slide. A man came out of a house that was tucked snug against a rugged hillside. Ada walked toward the water while Jessie and the man talked. She noticed a bald eagle perched on the top branch of a wind stripped evergreen.

After a few moments Jessie returned with a key and motioned Ada to follow. They walked up a trail to a one room cabin set back in the woods. Two twin beds with a nightstand separating them were on one side of the room; a sink, a small stove and a mini refrigerator were on the other. A fireplace took up most of the back wall filling the room with the sweet smell of burned wood. Ada was relieved to find a closet sized bathroom near the front door.

"There's no shower or bathtub," Ada said leaning out of the bathroom. Jessie pointed to a drain on the floor and a hand held nozzle hooked to the wall.

"When I first started coming here there wasn't a toilet or a sink just an old fashioned pump near the main cabin and a community outhouse."

"How old is this place?" Ada asked.

"Not that old," Jessie said laughing. "Stan and Caroline keep things simple so they don't get overrun with tourists. Just remember to put your clothes outside the door when you shower." Jessie took the bed closest to the cabin door. Ada looked in a large empty box beside the fireplace.

"Why don't you fill that. There are stacks of wood behind the cabin. Tonight will be a cold one," Jessie said.

The sound of the ocean blasting the rocks and then pulling back echoed all around. Ada found three waist high stacks of wood lining the back of the cabin. Everything was touched by a thin layer of moisture. Her black high tops, which were usually mouse quiet on the cement, crunched and squished against the layers of dead leaves and moss. The idea of city people vacationing here for peace and quiet made her laugh. The feel of city cement and steel seemed much safer than the slimy dampness of the forest, although getting away from the suffocating diesel smell was a much bigger draw. Her arms were full of wood when a hairy, black spider shot across the top piece. She squealed hurling the load to the ground and frantically brushed her clothes.

"I thought you guys might need this." A woman dressed in the same shades of grey as the man Jessie met on the path stood with a wheelbarrow and an ax.

"I didn't mean to startle you. My name's Caroline." She let go of the wheelbarrow and came forward with an outstretched hand. Ada looked at her own dirty hand as though a spider was hiding underneath the caked on mud but reluctantly offered it.

"I also came to invite Jessie and you to dinner tonight," the woman said smiling. "We haven't seen Jessie for over two years, lots of catching up to do." She leaned the ax against the wood stacks, "how about seven o'clock," she said over her shoulder as she disappeared around the corner.

It only took one trip to fill the box with the wheelbarrow. Jessie was sitting on a stool reading a newspaper at a table that folded down from the wall beside the sink.

"You're quick."

"That Caroline lady said to come to dinner at seven." Ada mentioned lying back on the bed with her headphones.

"You saw Caroline? You should've told her to come in and visit," Jessie said setting down the paper. "How'd she look?" she asked hindering Ada from listening to music.

"Like her husband minus the beard."

"I mean, was she healthy?" Sharing the same ability with Jessie was losing its novelty fast.

"Well actually," Ada snapped, "there's a lump in her left breast that she better get removed quick. How about you never ask me that again."

"Caroline is a good person." Jessie took a seat on the opposite bed. "We have the gift to see sickness and heal it. It's our duty to help those who suffer."

"I don't know anything about this woman. And who says it's my duty?"

"It's the right thing to do when you're capable of helping," Jessie said frustrated. "I know you know the difference between right and wrong. If someone slips and falls in front of you, would you help them up or just walk away?"

"Depends on the person," Ada retorted.

"You are your mother's daughter," Jessie said standing abruptly.

Ada felt the burning in her cheeks. "You're wrong, I'm nothing like my mother. I wouldn't leave my kid with a friend who dumps her in foster care."

"I thought it would be the safest place for you."

"Oh, I see. Where's the duty in that? No thought goes into healing strangers. It's just the right thing to do. What if one of those guys you think it's your duty to heal happens to be a sick pervert and the only thing that's keeping him from forcing himself on some girl is the pain and coughing from his rotting lungs, so you save the freak and screw over the girl?" She shoved her headphones in her pack and slipped it on.

"Ada, I'm sorry you've been exposed to such things," Jessie said softening her tone as Ada made her way to the door. "You can't mistrust all of humanity because of one person's failings. I could just as easily heal a person who helps kids in bad situations."

"Whatever! I don't believe in duty. I make my own

choices." Ada slammed the door behind her sending a group of birds fluttering into flight.

When it was time to go to dinner Jessie found Ada at the beach sitting in front of a fallen log listening to music.

She walked up slowly, "I know you must be starved. Tomorrow we'll walk to a food mart about a mile down the road and pick up some groceries, but for now Stan and Caroline are expecting us."

Ada stood without a word and followed. A long bridge that stretched just above the rocks and sand led up to a weathered wooden one story house. Glass ball floats hung in random clusters along the bridge and front porch. With all the rocks Ada couldn't imagine how the glass balls survived their arrival onto the beach. They passed a large window with a checkered pane where Ada caught a glimpse of Caroline with an arm full of dishes.

"Just relax, they are really nice people," Jessie said knocking on the door.

Caroline welcomed them into the front room where Ada stopped to take in an unbelievable amount of antiques. There wasn't an open space on any wall or table. Stan and Caroline seemed to like to collect anything that was old or slightly unique ranging from rusty tin boxes to strange looking rocks. She looked up and saw a plane made of wire hangers that stretched across a quarter of the front room's ceiling.

"Have a seat," Caroline said as she pointed to an open spot on the couch next to the oldest cat Ada had ever seen. Its fur was covered with the same layer of dust that blanketed everything in the room.

"Before we bought the cabins we owned a knick-knack shop in Victoria. Let me go out back and get Stan."

She disappeared into the kitchen.

Jessie turned to Ada with a stunned look, "you weren't kidding about the lump. I don't get you Ada. Have you no compassion?" Her disapproving head shake turned into a smile when Caroline re-entered with Stan and motioned them to come to the dinner table.

Ada managed to avoid small talk through dinner and busied herself looking at things as everyone made their way to the living room to talk about old times, until Jessie's voice turned serious.

"Caroline, you remember how I cured Stan's emphysema several years ago."

"We're so grateful for that; it's been a miracle. The doctors say his lungs are as healthy as a twenty-year-old runner."

"We take our walks and I don't even get breathless." Stan added stretching his arm across Caroline's shoulders.

"That's excellent," Jessie said smiling. "Now, I need to heal you Caroline."

Stan uncrossed his leg and came to the edge of the couch, "why, what's the matter? The doctor hasn't said there's anything wrong with her."

"Well it's been almost two years since I've seen a doctor Stan," Caroline said calmly. "For goodness sakes Jessie, whatever it is, I would be grateful for your help."

Ada set down a porcelain angel she was looking at to see just exactly what Jessie had to do to heal someone. Caroline moved across and sat next to Jessie. The cat that hadn't budged since they arrived slowly stood up, stretched and relocated onto Jessie's lap. Caroline laughed, lightening the mood. Jessie rested her hands on the upper part of Caroline's chest. Ada could feel tingling warmth that raised the hair on her arms. The house was silent except for the faint sound of waves in the background. Within seconds Ada could no longer sense the lump.

Jessie rested her hands on her lap causing the cat to jump to the ground and disappear into a back-room.

"The lump's gone," Jessie said.

"Along with my heartburn," Caroline laughed. "And I can't say I'll miss all the tests or doctor office visits."

"Too many miracles in one family triggers a visit from officials as well, something you don't need and I don't want," Jessie said standing to leave. "Thank you for a wonderful evening."

It took almost an hour to leave Stan and Caroline's, and only after agreeing to take a basket of food that would last a week.

"All you had to do was touch her. Did you have to think about it?" Ada asked as she avoided stepping on a small rodent that scurried across the ground.

The partially clouded moon offered a dim light for them to find their way.

"Oh yes, you have to focus your healing energy," she said flicking on a flashlight Stan had put in the basket. The woods loomed like black shadow. She didn't recognize the cabin until Jessie passed over it with the light. Thinking about the energy sent the warm tingling feeling through her body again.

"Can you bring people back from the dead?"

"No," Jessie laughed opening the cabin door. "I can't walk on water either."

Ada shivered. The air inside was as damp and cold as the outside. Jessie went straight for the fireplace.

"So, did you and my mom go around healing people together?"

"Definitely not," Jessie snorted contemptuously. "Your mother and I were friends at a different time in my life. Do you want to learn how to do this?" She said as she held up a piece of wood and crumpled newspaper.

"Sure." The lesson in fire starting ended Jessie answering any more questions Ada had about her mother or healing.

The following morning Jessie was gone before Ada got out of bed. Next to the basket of food she left a note that said she was making a few phone calls at the convenience store. She would be back in a couple of hours.

After Ada finished a banana and a roll, she checked her computer for the remote possibility of internet access. Nothing. She could hear the faint whoosh of waves and decided to explore the beach. She slipped on her sweatshirt and backpack as she closed the door behind her hoping to be long gone before Jessie showed up.

The sun was shining and the few clouds in the sky seemed frozen in place. She walked the opposite direction of the main house toward a narrow stretch of land covered with trees that pushed into the crowding water. The beach was empty until her eyes fell on a small silhouette stomping along in her direction. She almost lost her footing on one of the many slime covered rocks she was maneuvering across. The stomping silhouette turned into a little girl red faced and crying. On closer look Ada saw that she had a bloody, swollen lip.

"They're gonna kill that kitty!" she wailed without stopping when she noticed Ada staring at her.

Ada turned and looked in the direction the girl had come from. Barely visible, where the beach met the barrier of trees, she could see small figures bobbing up and down. They had to be kids; adults wouldn't bounce from place to place like that. She started in their direction.

The little girl's complaint made her remember the foster home she lived in when she was ten.

Margie was actually a decent foster mother. It was Joshua another kid Margie looked after that Ada had the problem with. He liked finding nests of newborn baby birds to use for batting practice. She winced remembering the one he had purposely lodged in her hair. She could still see the featherless limp body that had dropped from her tangles. She had laid it next to the steps where she sat for two hours waiting until Joshua dropped his metal bat to go inside for a bite to eat.

Picking up that bat was the reason for her first visit to the Between House. She went straight into the kitchen, and just as Joshua turned to face her, she slammed the bat down on top of his head, bringing him to his knees.

The three boys that were now shouting in front of her drowned out the memory of Margie's horrified screams. Ada reached down and snagged a good sized piece of drift wood. Squinting was no longer necessary. She was close enough to see that they were swinging a long piece of rope with something tied to the end, occasionally slamming it against the ground.

The shouting combined with the crashing of waves sounded like screeches from a strange flock of birds. When they finally noticed Ada, each boy jumped up on a rock near one another and glared down at her. She silently stood before them following the rope to a motionless handful of fur tied to the end.

"What are you staring at?" the tallest boy snapped following her gaze. "You don't belong here; you're just visiting. We live here so go somewhere else to see the ocean." The shorter boys who stood on rocks a little behind him muttered in agreement.

She stepped forward and swung the driftwood aiming for the tall boy's head as if it was a baseball destined to be a home run. The wood cut the wind like a swipe of a helicopter blade. Barely in time, he arched backwards falling off the rock and landing on his butt in the wet sand. With the driftwood in both hands Ada stared quietly at the bewildered boys.

"You could've killed me you psycho bitch!" He jumped to his feet with his friends at his side.

She took a small readied step forward.

"You can't be serious," he said, looking from her determined face to the piece of wood she held poised in her hands. "C'mon guys, let the freak have her spot."

Ada watched the boys disappear onto the trail in front of the main house before she turned to the kitten. Its pure black fur was damp with blood and the potent smell of a terrified animal. The injuries were too many to count, but it was a fighter. She could see labored breathing slightly move its chest. She pulled back her sleeves and gently touched its stomach. It croaked a muffled squeak, but kept its eyes closed. She laid both hands across its body leaving only the head and tail exposed.

"Okay, so focus," she said out loud.

The heat started in her bones and radiated out of her skin. Her entire core felt the awkward tickling numbness that a limb feels when it falls asleep. She opened her eyes to see if hot beads of sweat, or worse, blood, were pushing out of her pores, but the skin on her arms and hands looked normal. The more she focused the more the heat intensified. She felt that if she kept going she'd throw up, but she couldn't let go. The cat was still absorbing her energy, trying to fix the damage.

It was only seconds and the swollen body deflated. The pull of energy dwindled to nothing. She lifted her hands when she felt it struggling to free itself. It stood and gave a fluttering shake. She gently untied the rope from its middle as it enthusiastically rubbed the length of its body against her. Maybe being able to heal wasn't such a bad thing after all she thought as she ran her fingers against the kitten's cheek.

Ada roamed the beach, with the kitten she now called Samurai, until late afternoon, trying to think of reasons that might convince Jessie to let her keep it. Samurai followed closely as she walked toward the cabin.

"You saved it!"

The little girl with the swollen lip crawled out from under a worn out picnic table. Samurai ran to her like an old, lost friend.

"I thought he was dead," she said hugging the kitty tight as it rubbed its cheek against hers. Ada turned and started walking toward the cabin again.

"My mom and me live in the cabin way in the woods. Stan lets us live there cheap cause we can't see the ocean," the little girl said following close behind.

Ada noticed a light on in the cabin, and stopped in front of the door knowing Jessie would have to invite the girl in and ask a bunch of questions.

“Here’s your kitty,” the girl said holding the cat tight to her cheek.

“It’s not mine. It’s yours,” Ada said, facing the little girl waiting for her to leave. “Better go show your mom.”

She watched until the girl disappeared behind some trees and then slipped into the cabin.

5

The sun was barely up when Jessie and Ada started walking the path to the main road. Stan was waiting at the mouth of the woods with a brown bag full of fruit and sandwiches. He lingered around until the taxi showed up. Ada stayed close trying to hear mention of where they were going next and hoped it wasn't another suffocating hospital, but as usual Jessie was secretive and revealed nothing. They were fifteen minutes into the taxi ride when Jessie broke the silence.

"I found this in front of the door this morning." She handed Ada a wrinkled piece of construction paper folded into a small square. Ada opened it and found a stick figure with the same long, brown hair as the little girl from the beach standing next to a small, black cat each with a hand and paw raised waving goodbye. She slipped it into the small pocket on the front of her backpack and lay back closing her eyes until the taxi came to a stop again at the docks.

On the ferry back to Vancouver they ate the food Stan had packed. When the ferry docked, Jessie hurried off toward a destination only she knew, while Ada strolled behind letting blocks separate them.

Deep into a residential area she caught up to Jessie waiting in front of an old stone building with *Sanatorium1865* carved on the front.

"Don't tell me this is some kind of insane asylum," Ada said dropping her duffle bag on the ground.

"No, it's actually for people who are chronically ill," Jessie said opening the gate. She glanced back and found Ada staring at her with crossed arms, not budging.

"Oh great, more sick people, which means more weird smells," she said, noticing a figure in the window.

"Do you think any of these people are happy about being sick?" Jessie snapped. "Instead of complaining, you could help."

"I'm waiting out here," Ada said stubbornly.

"Not out front. There's a yard around back."

The building was small compared to the park that stretched out behind it. Ada walked to the farthest end away from the hospital and sat down against the trunk of a weeping willow. A fence separated her from another building's parking lot. The willow's dangling leaves almost touched the ground on her side, but on the other side someone had given it a severe pruning. She leaned back against the tree and plugged a headphone in.

A strange whining hum broke the silence. She peeked around the trunk and spotted a boy in an electric wheel chair coming straight toward her.

"What now?" she sighed listening to the hum as it grew louder and louder. She pulled her legs in close hoping she wasn't spotted.

"You picked the worst corner. The other side has a stream." The boy said bringing his wheelchair to a stop next to Ada.

"Just trying to listen to music," she answered holding up the iPod long enough that a butterfly landed on top of it.

"What the..." She flicked her wrist sending the butterfly back into flight. The cold shoulder wasn't as convincing with butterflies floating around. He laughed at her reaction and quickly stopped when he noticed her glare.

"I saw you with the lady who's helping people inside." He paused a moment. "Can you do what she does?"

She could feel his gaze on the side of her face anticipating an answer. Plucking the headphone from her ear she turned toward him. He seemed around her age or possibly a little older. His muscular upper body magnified the sunken look of his jeans.

"What do you mean?" she asked annoyed.

He moved closer to the fence staring silently at the parking lot. Usually Ada appreciated uncomfortable silence, but after a couple minutes she felt the urge to find another spot in the front of the building.

"I've been here for ten years and in this for eleven." He patted the arm of the wheelchair. "You see, next year I'll be eighteen and old enough to function on my own.

I've been working out and everything, getting ready, but they say no matter what, from here down," he pointed to the base of his stomach not turning to see if Ada was even looking, "is never going to work again. I remember everything like it just happened. We were driving back from getting groceries, me, my mom and my little sister. A red truck was sitting at the stop sign waiting for his chance to pullout, and right as we're sailing past he pulls out smack into the side of us. Seat belts were never a big deal on our small town roads. I remember the glass swirling around in the car as it rolled to a crashing stop against a tree. My mom's banged up face telling me it would be okay faded in and out. At that point I couldn't feel any part of my body. I saw the fire and then everything went black. They told me later that my mom lifted the car up enough so someone could pull me from underneath. Then, she came and laid next to me and my sister and died before the ambulance could get there."

"Why are you telling me all this?" Ada asked staring at his profile.

"If a hundred and thirty pound woman can lift a two ton car," he paused, "maybe the lady you came here with can help me. They say it will be hard enough for me to help myself let alone a thirteen-year-old girl." He turned his wheelchair to face her. "My sister's been in foster care as long as I've been in here. I've only seen her twice since the accident. If I could get out of this thing, I could help her."

"Believe me, if she says she can't do it," Ada said, nodding toward the doors of the building where Jessie was, "then she can't do it." She stood and brushed at the dampness on her jeans left from sitting in the grass. She knew from her own experience with foster care that his sister could use the help. "But let me try."

He turned his chair toward her. "You have the power too?"

She sensed the injury in the center of his spine, but couldn't understand why Jessie was unable to help until she rested her hands on his legs. It felt like there was only a thin layer of skin clinging to the frail bones. The energy that coursed through the kitten was strong compared to the weak trickle in his legs. Everything from the injury down seemed to barely exist, but just above the energy radiated. She closed her eyes and focused all of her attention on the energy above the injury trying to pull it downward. Her temperature surged. Her hands started to burn. She couldn't tell whether she was actually helping him or starting to spontaneously combust. Neither of them noticed the frantic approach of Jessie and Joseph.

"Ada! We have to go!" Jessie said grabbing her arm and dragging her toward an opening in the parking lot fence.

"My stuff!" Ada said pulling back before noticing that Joseph had her things. She looked back at the boy.

His alarmed expression caused her to follow his gaze to the building. Several men in suits were rushing from the double doors pointing and yelling in her direction. Over the top of the building swooped a helicopter that hovered in front of them. Ada raced after Jessie slipping through the fence opening. The helicopter caused leaves and dust to swirl around them.

A green SUV squealed to a stop almost running over Ada's toes. She started to run in a different direction when Joseph grabbed her arm and shoved her and her bags into the SUV. A man Ada recognized from the first hospital was driving. They flew across the grass slamming over a cement curb onto the main road. Ada fastened her seatbelt before she bounced her head off of the ceiling. The ominous thumping roar of the helicopter hovered just above. She looked out the back window expecting to see someone following them, but there were only the cars they passed, shrinking into the background. The sharp turns pressed her back and forth between Jessie and the door.

"We're hitting rush hour!" the driver yelled. "There's a traffic tunnel just ahead. If you get out inside you may have a chance to lose the helicopter."

"They aren't looking for you Ada," Jessie said writing something on a small piece of paper, tucking it in a roll of money that she pressed into Ada's hand. "Meet me in two hours at this place."

"We're separating?" Ada gasped.

"He'll let you out at the beginning of the tunnel. Wait a few minutes and then go back out the way we came in. From there you can find your way to that place." She patted Ada's hand. "He'll drop me off at the opposite end where they're expecting us to come out. If I'm not at the place in two hours call Gretchen."

"No way. I'm staying with you. Let the empty car go through they'll follow it," Ada said, growing flustered as the tunnel ahead got closer.

"I've endangered you. I'm sorry. I know the senator. He'll do whatever it takes to capture a healer. He believes we're the closest thing to the fountain of youth." A short way into the tunnel Jessie had the driver edge through traffic and pull over to the side.

"See that?" She pointed to a dark alcove in the tunnel wall. "Tuck yourself in there for a few minutes. Don't stay on the freeway." She pushed a reluctant Ada out of the car and then disappeared deeper into the tunnel.

Ada hid in the sooty alcove checking a door barely visible except for the grimy handle only to find it locked. The car exhaust turned the air into a toxic mist, forcing her to hold her breath. After a few moments she rushed toward the tunnel opening until she reached open air.

She scanned the sky expecting to see the helicopter but it was nowhere in sight. The continuous rush of air from passing cars pushed and pulled threatening to knock her off of the narrow sidewalk. She put on her backpack and walked quickly holding her duffle bag out in front of her, until she came to the end of the cement wall that trapped her on the freeway. Not far from the tunnel she ended up on a somewhat quieter street.

There wasn't a person around to ask if she was anywhere near her destination. Jessie's paper had an address with a small hand drawn map of the surrounding streets. The street she was on didn't match any of the names on the map. She found a bus stop sign and sat down to wait.

Old houses that had been turned to small businesses lined the street. A yellow car with taxi written on the side pulled up in front of the bus stop. A man with blonde, feathered hair and mirrored sunglasses rolled down his window.

"Where you headed?" he asked smiling.

Ada looked at the illuminated sign on top of his car that read taxi, and the rates that were listed on the back passenger door.

"Don't worry about that," he said noticing her eyes on the rates. "I'll cut you a deal; trust me, it'll be faster than what you're waiting for." He nodded toward the bus stop sign.

It seemed too convenient, but it looked like the same type of taxi that had picked them up in front of Stan and Caroline's. She fished the paper from her pocket.

"Denman near Haro." She wasn't about to give anyone the exact address.

"Back roads, twenty minutes, twenty bucks." He grinned, "believe me, the bus will take you an hour."

Jessie had given her the roll of money, so the faster she got there the better, she figured.

"Alright." She started to get in the back with her things.

He opened his door to step out, "let me put your stuff in the trunk."

"No." Ada shook her head.

"Okay," he laughed closing the door for her.

The cab was meticulously kept, not a speck of dust on the dashboard. She noticed pictures of a girl and boy taped above the CD player. They looked like twins with their black hair and dark complexions.

"So what grade are you in?" he asked.

She pretended not to hear his question and watched the buildings blur by the window.

"I probably wouldn't be driving this cab for a living if I'd done better in school." He laughed awkwardly glancing at Ada in the mirror.

She tried to block out the cab driver's ramblings, but seeing him constantly peering at her in the rearview mirror made her uneasy.

"Not much further and we'll be there."

From the crack that ran up the middle of the backseat Ada noticed a small white card sticking halfway out. When she reached for it, it popped out the rest of the way landing on the seat. She picked it up and held it down by her lap to have a look. It read: Janak Kapoor, Vancouver Taxi Service, along with several telephone numbers.

She looked in the mirror to find the cab driver scrutinizing her.

"Everything okay?" he asked.

"Yep," she said gazing out the window until he stopped staring.

She looked at the card again. The guy driving sure didn't look like a Janak Kapoor. She flipped it over. On the back, in scratchy writing, were the words "Help Me." Her heart skipped a beat. She didn't dare look up until she could swallow down her panic.

"You falling asleep back there or something?"

"How could I with your constant babble." She glared directly at the mirror until he laughed and looked away.

"You aren't offending me. I like feisty," he said keeping his eyes on the road.

She tried to squeeze her hand through the crack without moving her upper body too much. Her arm was half way in before the tips of her fingers felt sweaty skin. There was movement and then fingers were brushing hers. She felt around until she came across what ended up being his wrists bound by duct-tape. It took a moment to find the corner of the tape, and then slowly she pulled and worked until his hands were free. The car began to slow down.

"Here we are," the driver said pulling to the curb across from a fancy brick apartment building. A man in a suit was standing on the sidewalk watching them park. She scanned the area for a way out.

The apartment building was situated on a steep hillside overlooking a wooded area. On her side of the street it was an open field. She was sure to get caught if she tried to outrun two men through an open field.

"Get it moving back there. What are you doing?" he snapped opening her car door.

"I have to pay you don't I?"

"Actually, don't worry about that. Someone else has already paid your fare." He laughed.

"So this isn't Denman Street?" She stalled looking out the window while slipping on her backpack. The only thing that caught her eye was a parking garage under the building where a mechanical arm raised and lowered to let cars in and out.

"Quit stalling and get out of the car."

The man in the suit was now standing on the sidewalk next to the imposter cabdriver. She knew if she went inside with them she was finished. It would be almost impossible to get away. She backed out keeping her head in the car while she pulled her duffle bag toward her. On the side of the seat she noticed a lever that pulled the seat down opening the back of the car to the trunk.

"I hope you're ready," she said aloud.

"Move it."

As she was yanked out of the car she grabbed her bag and the lever. Instantly the man in the trunk burst out of the backseat yelling and thrashing his arms, knocking down the man in the suit.

Ada bolted for a spot to hide that would give her a chance to sneak away, but the phony cabdriver was already after her. She hurled her duffle bag at his legs sending him face first to the cement, and then ran into the parking garage.

It was packed with cars, plenty of places to hide, but how would she get out? The walls facing the street and hillside were covered with large glassless windows. She crouched low peeking around cars to see what was happening, but could only hear voices. She moved toward the wall facing the hillside to put as much space as possible between her and the men.

"Forget him! We need to find the girl."

"911, Police!" echoed from down the road. It was the man from the trunk. She heard the shuffle of feet and peeked around a car to see where they were. They were standing not far from the mechanical arm. She also noticed an exit door diagonally across the garage from her.

"Call the senator. We gotta get her upstairs before the cops show up."

She couldn't make out what the guy in the suit was saying into his cell phone, but she knew more people were on their way. She made sure to stay behind tires, so they couldn't find her by looking under cars. The exit was too far and the street was too open. She edged her way to the windows. A large, white van hid her while she scouted the hillside for a possible escape route. It was almost steep enough to pass as a cliff littered with rocks and shrubs. At the bottom was a chain link fence. She heard more voices echo through the garage and the faint sound of sirens.

The men fell silent as a sharp tapping sound grew louder. Ada got down on all fours to see what was happening. A pair of shiny black shoes and the bottom half of a silver plated cane came to a halt across the garage from her. The shoes of the other two men scurried past as if following orders from the man with the cane.

"Hello young lady, I'm Senator Herald Grimes. I just want to ask you a few questions. No one's going to hurt you."

The shuffle of shoes sounded in every direction. They were surrounding her. There was only one way to go. She climbed onto the window edge and turned so she was facing the garage. She intended to climb down holding onto shrubs and tufts of grass, but she slipped and lost her grip. Trying to turn to her side sent her into a speeding roll straight down the hill.

A chain link fence brought her to a sudden, painful stop. She lay flat on her back staring at the cloud covered sky. A crow with a white wrapper hanging from its beak flew overhead. She looked around when she heard sirens wailing somewhere on the streets above. Her whole body ached but her right leg throbbed. A thick, rusty, stray piece of wire sticking out of the fence was sunk deep into her right calf. She sat up carefully to assess the damage. Looking at it made her nauseous.

She tore the rip in her pants wider so she could see if it punctured through to the other side of her calf. A black and blue lump bulged where the wire was trying to exit.

Voices from the street above reminded her to

move faster. She noticed a white haired man watching her from the garage window and knew by his intense stare that it was the senator. The others were probably on their way down. She grabbed the wire with one hand and used the other to press against her calf. Blood was pooling and leaking little streams where the wire entered her leg. The dragging feeling as she pulled the wire out made her look away. The old man was now holding up his cell phone trying to take a picture of her.

"Weirdo," she grunted pulling the wire the rest of the way out. Blood gushed between her fingers as she applied pressure to stop the bleeding. A cold sweat and watering mouth from nauseousness made her want to lay back and stare at the sky.

"You wanted to see if you could heal yourself," she mumbled aloud.

Pressing both hands on each side of her calf, she focused on the damage and tried to pull energy from all over her body, directing it to the puncture wound. The burning, stabbing pain changed to a tingling itch. Without looking she could see every step of the healing process unfolding in her mind. Heat flushed the skin around the injury until it felt numb.

She moved her hands to see, only blood was left, not even a scar. She used her sweatshirt sleeve to wipe the area clean.

The senator was still watching as she found an opening in the chain link fence and squeezed through. Not far from the fence, a winding path brought her into the middle of a busy park. As she walked she tried to straighten herself up wiping away dirt and fixing her hair, but the tear in her pants was too ridiculous. For the first time it was a relief not to be alone. She kept looking over her shoulder. She knew they would eventually show up.

The old man's intense stare emanated a relentless obsession. The thought of him taking her picture when she removed the rusty wire made her shiver. She had to find the café, at least to warn Jessie. Downtown would be the safest place to start, full of people, and no one's paying attention unless something gets out of hand.

6

Downtown Vancouver was the bustling city of solitude Ada was used to. Streets packed with people who would keep to themselves unless provoked by some unforeseen disturbance.

Ada ducked into a second hand store and bought a pair of sewing scissors and turned her jeans into shorts, rolling them twice to hide her crooked cutting. She didn't mind that her duffle bag was gone. It only had clothes in it. On the floor next to the register she reorganized her backpack to fit an extra pair of jeans she had bought. A clerk drew a map leading to the café on Denman Street where she was supposed to meet Jessie. She didn't have long to wait.

Staying out of sight was easy on a Friday. She kept close to buildings and stood in door wells looking for anyone suspicious. After a few minutes of watching, everyone looked suspicious. A group of people laughing over coffee seemed too noisy, a woman in a black shawl dropped her purse too conveniently, a delivery man on a bike stopped at the end of the sidewalk to check an invoice; everyone seemed suspicious. Ada angrily stepped out of the door well and crossed the street brushing past the front tire of the delivery man's bike. She wasn't about to spend her life hiding in door wells or broom closets.

Ada knew the café was close when she stepped up on a curb under a sign marked Denman Street. She scanned the shops along both sides of the street to see if one was the café. Diagonally across from her a noisy group of people formed a roped in line along an old brick building. Two oversized bouncers stood in front of black double doors occasionally letting one or two people from the line go inside.

Watching the people, she didn't notice the black car recklessly changing lanes until it was too late. It pulled up to the curb in front of her almost knocking her back. For a brief second she was face to face with the older man who was watching her from the window of the apartment garage. He grabbed her arm through the car window and yanked her toward him while a man in the backseat flung open the door. Ada pulled her arm free, swinging herself into the back door managing to slam it closed, giving herself the moment she needed to escape.

She darted across the street just missing oncoming traffic and shifted past the bouncers as they were letting a couple through the doors. A long staircase, painted as dark as a night sky, with strings of colored lights to guide the way, led downward. The walls and floor vibrated to the pounding bass of deafening music. She looked back to see the bouncers holding up her stalkers. It wouldn't take long for them to wheedle their way inside she thought speeding up her pace.

The end of the stairs led into an enormous warehouse, dim except for the flashing lights. There was barely standing room. She squeezed sideways into the crowd. The air was moist with the smell of cigarettes, alcohol and sweat. It was like opening a garbage can on a hot summer day. She slowly made her way around the dance floor to the back of the club when the lights snapped on and a voice boomed through the speakers. Everyone stopped in confusion.

"Sorry to alarm you folks, but there is an underage kid roaming the bar. As soon as she is located and brought to the front, the music and drinks will start again."

To Ada's horror, on a giant screen that once displayed dancing people, a picture of her head and upper torso appeared looming over the crowd. She recognized the chain link fence in the background.

"If you see her, hold on to her; someone will be around to help," the voice boomed from above.

Ada noticed closed doors behind a stack of speakers. She quickly slipped through them before anyone had a chance to connect her face to the one in the projection. A long corridor led her to an unlocked door. She opened it slowly. It was packed with stacks of metal barrels and cardboard boxes. In the far corner of the room was an open door leading outside.

"You can't be in here. This is off limits." A dark haired man with a strong accent grumbled as he seized her by the arm. His grip was too tight to break free.

A large tattoo on his forearm of a praying Virgin Mary stared sympathetically. Across the bottom of the tattoo was a gaping gash that could have used stitches.

"Wait, Please! I just need out of here." Ada laid her free hand over the cut. The man shook his head and started dragging her toward the hallway. She quickly pulled her hand away. The wound was gone.

"Madre de Dios." He dropped her arm with a startled expression making the sign of the cross then searching his arm for the cut. The speakers echoed the same message as before silencing the rumbling crowd. Ada glanced nervously at the hallway expecting the senator and his henchmen to appear.

"Go," he pointed to the open back door. "Turn left when you get out there." He motioned her to move quickly then went to the door that led to the nightclub and closed and locked it.

Ada stepped out to a dark alley and went left like he said. After a few blocks of darkness and a startling moment discovering three drunks covered with newspapers, she came out on a different street altogether.

It didn't take long to find Denman Street and the café. A few people sat at tables, but no Jessie. Ada quickly walked in, took a seat in a back corner, and waited. After an hour of watching people passing in and out the door, she bought a lemonade, so she didn't feel like she was loitering. Counting drips that slid down her sweating glass of lemonade, and looking up when the bells jingled on the front door, was how she passed the time. At ten o'clock the barista started stacking chairs and wiping counters.

"You waiting on a ride or something," the barista asked Ada with a smile.

"Someone's supposed to meet me here," Ada said picking up her backpack that was leaning against the leg of her chair.

"It'll take me another half hour to close up if you want to wait," she said flicking a switch that turned off the illuminated "open" sign.

"Thank you," Ada said staring at the door wishing she could will Jessie to step through it.

It seemed the barista took her time closing up, but eventually, when she had her purse and keys in hand she motioned Ada to the front door and watched sympathetically as Ada stepped out onto the sidewalk.

"Hey, do you need a ride?" she asked while locking the coffee shop door. Out on the street Ada looked in all directions expecting the senator and his men to show up and try to shove her in their car.

"No, I..." Ada noticed a sign pointing the way to the ocean. "I don't have far to go. Thanks though." She walked quickly in the direction the sign was pointing. Downtown was safe to disappear in during the day, but deadly, or worse at night.

Ada located the same log in front of the ivy covered hotel. The darkness hid the bay making it a black abyss except for a sprinkle of lights from ships and the sound of the pushing and pulling of waves. This was one of the few spots she knew in this country and she was hoping, if Jessie wasn't captured, that she would think to come back and check.

Her sweatshirt was stretched down around her legs, but the damp ocean air was frigid. She tucked up against the log and burrowed down in the sand. It was impossible to sleep for fear that the ocean would creep up and reclaim the log and her along with it. The few night strollers were long gone when she decided to look inside the hotel.

Instead of relaxing, the warmth made her sway with exhaustion as she read the plaques telling the hotel's history. It was past midnight; a young girl in the lobby alone would look suspicious, so she went straight for the bathroom. Ada tiptoed to the last stall, latched the door as best she could, and hung her backpack on a hook on the door. She sat down on the back of the toilet and pulled her legs up resting her feet on the seat. The automatic flusher went off twice before she made herself comfortable and dozed off staring at the water in the bowl.

Ada woke up to the sound of something rolling to a stop in front of the stall door. Before she could stand the door shook and then burst open causing her to slip off of the toilet into the corner.

"Good Lord!" A woman with a mop in hand yelled when she noticed Ada tucked to the side of the toilet. Ada jumped to her feet grabbing her backpack while the woman shook her head disapprovingly.

"Rent a room next time or stay the hell out!" the woman said, not budging as Ada tried to squeeze past. She accidently caught her foot on the bucket and turned it over. Water and curse words followed her out of the bathroom.

She dried her feet on the carpet, straightened her clothes in the hallway and then walked quietly into the lobby where she busied herself pretending to look at brochures. The front desk man seemed too absorbed in his book to notice her. It was only four in the morning, so Ada tried to stretch her time in the warmth by looking at every pamphlet.

Her heart jumped when she pulled up the brochure about the suspension bridge Jessie had said they would visit. The man at the front desk cleared his throat objectionably loud, so she took the brochure and went just outside the door.

She hadn't checked her computer since the fall down the hillside. It was a relief when the screen popped up, and a non-secure cable connection allowed her internet access. She discovered that the bridge was an hour away by bus and a bus stop was just a few blocks from the hotel.

Another loud throat clearing made her turn and face the front desk man standing in the doorway with crossed arms. She stuffed her computer in her backpack, returning his cold stare.

"Get tired of reading?" she said rolling her eyes as she slipped on her pack.

She sat on a log feeling the warmth of the sunrise on her back. The suspension bridge wouldn't open until nine. All Ada could do was hope that Jessie would remember wanting to visit the bridge before they left.

At seven in the morning the restaurant at the bottom of the hotel opened for breakfast. The smell of baked rolls made Ada's legs weak with hunger. She hadn't eaten since yesterday morning, so she decided to order as much as she could to the astonishment of the server.

After stuffing herself on strawberry crepes, she found her way to the bus, which quickly filled with morning commuters. Ada pressed her forehead against the window and watched the buildings dwindle to dense forest.

"It's beautiful, isn't it? This route takes longer, but it's the only way I like to start my day." A woman next to her said. Ada pretended not to hear. The woman probably thought the creeping darkness around her vision was just old age, but Ada could see it was more. It wasn't that she was "antisocial" like Gretchen had written in her file. Being face to face with sickness was like talking to someone with a large piece of food stuck in their teeth or a booger hanging out of their nose.

She learned young that bringing up a health problem was the same as talking about what people do on the toilet. She watched the woman get off the bus. If it wasn't for the pressure damage in the woman's eyes Ada wouldn't have known which person it was that spoke to her. She thought about what Jessie might have done, put her hands on a stranger? She shook her head at the thought. Putting her hands on a rabid dog seemed safer.

The bus dropped her off in front of the park. Ada watched it pull away wondering if Jessie would remember their talk about the bridge or was this just going to be a sightseeing trip. She waited in line to buy her ticket behind a couple and a family with three small children running circles around everyone. There were a few people scattered around the front, but no Jessie.

Ada followed a densely treed trail that led her to the mouth of the suspension bridge. It sagged like a jump rope across an open lush ravine. There was a waist high chain link fence running along each side of the bridge so that when the bridge swayed people wouldn't be launched to their deaths. The flooring was made up of planks bound together by cables that were flexible and could move side to side or roll like a wave. The family from the front gate waddled onto the bridge in single file; only the parents could stretch their arms long enough to hold onto each side of the fencing. The children skipped and jumped down the center without a care while the bridge bounced back and forth as they crossed.

No thanks, Ada thought to herself. She wasn't afraid of reasonable heights, but being dangled in midair above pointy tree tops and a rushing river was too much.

She sat down on a bench tucked in the trees and

dug out her iPod. People filtered on and off the bridge but still no Jessie. When she got tired of sitting she stood near the opening of the bridge and counted people or made a hopeless attempt at finding an internet connection. The hours trickled by.

At two in the afternoon Ada shoved her iPod into her backpack. Three hours and the park would close. She watched as a group of girls her age started across the bridge laughing and pointing into the ravine. When an older couple with canes headed out onto the bridge, she decided she had to try. Being afraid was annoying and it would be embarrassing to tell Jessie that she went to the park and didn't cross the bridge or even step out onto it.

She made sure no one was behind her and then stepped softly onto the planks, holding tight to both rails. She kept reminding herself that people had been crossing all day and the bridge had held strong. A quarter of the way out she heard the excited shouts of children coming behind her. Ada grabbed the rail on one side of the bridge with both hands and braced herself. It creaked and moaned bouncing like a boat hitting choppy water. She held tight and watched the ground below swing back and forth.

The kids rushed past as she gulped down a mouthful of saliva to keep from throwing up. Healing offered little help, because each sway of the bridge brought a new wave of nausea.

She'd climbed tall trees and even sat on the rooftop

ledge of a three story junior high school and never felt like this. She rested her forehead against the hand rail. The ground was so far away she expected to see clouds forming around the bridge.

"I was hoping you would remember our plans to visit this place."

Ada looked up to find Jessie standing next to her admiring the scenery.

"You don't know how glad I am to see you," Ada said trying to straighten up. "Now let's get off this bridge."

They returned to the bench Ada had spent most of the day on. Once she was on solid ground the shaky sick feeling was gone.

"There were people following me. I couldn't meet you at the café, or I would have ended up bringing them right to you," Jessie said reassuringly.

"Don't worry they brought themselves to me." Ada took her backpack off and sat it at her feet while Jessie looked around frantically. "I lost them. Seriously, I lost them," Ada reassured.

"That complicates things." Jessie stood and paced in front of the bench. "I'm sorry Ada, this is why I've stayed away."

"So, who's Senator Grimes?"

Jessie stopped pacing and stared at Ada, "you met the senator?"

"He introduced himself while I was trying to jump out a garage window. Does that count as meeting?" Ada explained all that happened since their separation. Jessie was especially interested in how quickly Ada was able to heal such a deep puncture wound.

"No one saw you heal yourself, did they?"

Ada paused for a moment, "I didn't have a lot of options. I couldn't have run off with a big wire jabbed into my leg."

Jessie started pacing again. "Who do you think saw you?"

"I don't think, I know that senator guy saw me. He took pictures with his phone. I guess I forgot to mention the night club ordeal."

"Jesus Ada," she pulled at the top of her hair. "Out of all the people to see you heal, he's the worst."

"I wasn't trying to screw things up. It's not like I'm used to being hunted. What's his problem anyways?"

"He's a man who believes that money can buy anything or anyone. I worked for him for a short time." Jessie sat down again and started digging through her purse. "It's not something I'm proud of."

"You don't seem like the politician type."

"I wasn't a politician. I used to demand money for healing people, large amounts of money."

She pulled a small leather booklet from her purse.

"Really?" Ada hadn't thought of this possibility. "How much money did people pay you?"

Jessie turned and faced her with a serious expression. "Most people will give everything they have to be rid of a painful disease, and some people will do anything to ensure a few more days of life. The senator started wanting visits everyday even when he was healthy. He had people follow me everywhere and then he decided that I wasn't allowed to heal anyone else but him."

She stared quietly into the woods for a few moments. "I realized I was being just like the senator. He was hoarding my healing and I was hoarding money. So I went into hiding and now I help who I want to, when I can."

"And he just won't give up?"

Jessie gave a weary nod, "and now he knows you're a healer."

Ada hadn't given it much thought, but the senator did see her heal the puncture wound; so did that mean he'd be lurking around trying to catch her, forever? She looked up to see if there were any suspicious onlookers.

"I wish I could tell you he was the only one looking for our kind. Most people have no idea we exist, but there are numerous organizations that know we're very real and would like to get their hands on us." She leafed through the pages of the booklet not settling on any one page. "It starts out as a few tests, and then you want to leave and they tell you with a big smile that you're now property of the common good, too many people would benefit from your ability, and before you know it, you're a prisoner and no one's getting help." Jessie stopped abruptly and sat silent, staring at a page in the little leather booklet.

Seeing Jessie so upset made Ada feel her new found talent was more of a curse. How would she be able to enjoy anything if she was always on the run?

"Sorry to sound so somber. There's always a bright side." She smiled pressing the leather booklet into Ada's hand. "I saved a large amount of money for you. I meant to give it to you when you were a little older and ready to start a path in life, but considering the circumstances I want you to have access to money. I also wrote down an email address I can be reached at. Sometimes it takes me a few days, but I do check it with some regularity."

Ada stared at the page full of numbers.

"The account numbers are here, and those are the pin numbers." She flipped to the back of the book, and pulled out a small key tucked behind the leather sleeve. "This is to a safety deposit box at this bank. If you're responsible, you'll never have to worry about money again."

Ada held the booklet open in disbelief. "Why are you doing all of this for me? We're not even related and you don't seem that close to my mom."

"I never wanted kids and yet somehow our paths crossed. Things happen for a reason; I never ignore that," Jessie said patting Ada's knee.

"Well... thanks." Ada tucked the booklet in her back pocket. "Things have gotten really weird since we've met, but I'm glad I know you." She looked at the ground hating the awkward moment.

Jessie checked her wrist watch, "we should get

going. I have an appointment in Portland tomorrow and we're going to need to prepare."

"Not more sick people," Ada groaned sliding on her backpack. An old woman struggling onto the bridge turned and gave them an appalled look.

"You know, a little sympathy isn't a bad thing. And, no I won't be helping any sick people tomorrow. The appointment is with a scientist friend of mine. He's a good man. If you ever needed help, he's someone you could trust."

They took the bus to a shopping center where Jessie picked out a couple different shades of hair color and tried holding fake hair swatches up to Ada's face before Ada managed to wander off down a different aisle. She bought some necessities that she wouldn't consider buying from a second hand store and met Jessie at the front counter.

They found a broken down motel like the one they'd stayed in when they had first arrived. There was internet access so Ada was comfortably set up on the bed when Jessie emerged from the bathroom with orange hair. She tossed Ada a baseball cap.

"Try that on. I wouldn't know where to begin with hair as dark and long as yours."

"I'm glad. I like my hair color," Ada said putting on the cap.

7

It was late afternoon when their bus arrived in Portland. The trip from Vancouver was quiet and smooth except for the downpour. One overflowing cloud seemed to stretch all the way from Seattle to Portland.

From the bus station they walked to Jessie's appointment. Her new hair color had mixed with the rain and left orange streaks dribbling down the sides of her face staining her shirt collar. She snapped at Ada for not telling her, but knowing the rain of the Northwest Ada figured it would run clean eventually.

After trekking a large hill they stood in front of a university hospital. To Ada's relief the appointment was in the university section. Jessie dried the water from her face but was stuck with an orange tint. They went up a few flights of stairs before they arrived at a door marked "Lab 1 Prof. Strathern." Jessie lightly knocked at the door then opened it and peeked in.

"He's usually in the back," she whispered over her shoulder to Ada. They entered a room with empty desks and chairs. Jessie seemed to know her way so Ada followed. She led her into another room filled with long counters cluttered with equipment, beakers filled with an assortment of liquids, and strange utensils strung out everywhere. Ada noticed a man in the back of the room hunched over the eye piece of a large microscope.

"Let's wait until he sits up. I don't want to startle him." But Jessie's whisper caused Professor Strathern to turn around squinting to see who was there as he fumbled for his glasses.

"Jessie!" he gasped and immediately stood and started toward them with outstretched arms. "It's been too long." He was a tall, grey haired man with blue, grey eyes that never seemed to stop smiling or squinting.

"We've had some troubles with the senator." She nodded toward Ada.

"Oh my, she is a spitting image of Simone, isn't she?" He held out a weathered but remarkably steady hand. Ada hesitated and then slowly offered hers.

"I promise I won't bite," he laughed and patted her on the back. "I only knew your mother a short time, but she's one of those people who make a lasting impression." For a brief moment the smile left his eyes when he heard voices outside the door.

"I hope you were careful coming up here. I also have had the misfortune of a visit from our former associate. I'm too old to do much good going up against his young hooligans." The voices moved on. Professor Strathern pulled up three chairs in the back of his lab and he and Jessie settled into a deep conversation.

After glancing at the equipment and tools scattered around, Ada sat down at a desk a few feet away and listened, hoping to hear a little more about her mother, but nothing was said.

"Well ladies, I think it's dinner time. I would be honored if you would stay at my home. I'll order out."

Ada drifted behind as they talked nonstop, apparently making up for lost time.

She followed Jessie and the professor up a path to an old two story Victorian house. The vegetation threatened to swallow everything. Vines crawled up tree trunks and across the face of the house. Around the back Ada stopped to take in a bay window trimmed in stained glass. It didn't seem like a house a scientist would live in, but more like an old woman who liked to grow things. Inside was similar to the outside except that all the vegetation was recreated in stained glass that hung everywhere.

"A hobby of mine, but I'm running out of places to put them." He picked up a phone. "Do you like pizza Ada?"

She paused and stared surprised by the question, "yeah, sure, food's food."

"It's amazing how like your mother you are. You know I spent several months with her." A voice on the other end of the phone drew his attention away.

Ada walked outside along the wrap-a-round porch until she found a chair tucked back in a corner. The rain pattered against leaves sounding as if a hundred umbrellas were open in the gloomy yard. She stared out into the darkness thinking how weird it was that Professor Strathern knew more about her mother than she did.

"I have something for you," Professor Strathern said, emerging from around the corner. He handed Ada a folder. She laid it on her lap remembering her own file filled with someone else's version of the defining moments in her life. She opened to a notebook sized picture of a group of people standing in front of the bay window. A tall, dark haired woman in an elegant skirt and blouse stood in the middle staring off into the distance.

"That's her," Ada said taking a closer look at the photo.

"Are these the first photos you've received of your mother?" Professor Strathern asked kneeling down next to her.

Ada ignored the question, and pulled out the next picture. This time it was her mother with a dark haired man in a fancy suit.

"That would be Jean Mechan, your mother's fiancé." He tapped on the face of the man in the picture. "Quite a businessman as well as a brilliant biochemist. He's made a fortune in pharmaceuticals."

Ada flipped back to the previous picture to see if he was in it. There he was again, standing next to her mother, but the suit was hidden by a lab coat. Ada was surprised to recognize the man next to him.

"The senator," she said looking closer. "He looks

even weirder without the grey hair."

"This is about twenty years ago, not to mention he had Jessie healing him every day," Professor Strathern said laughing. "I'm sorry you've had the misfortune of meeting him."

"Yeah me too, he's a real weirdo."

"You're a good judge of character Ada; regrettably I wasn't. You see, the senator and Dr. Mechan were funding our team, and quite a team it was, all leading minds in their fields. We were trying to find the source to Jessie and your mother's healing abilities. The goal was to create a vaccine that would stimulate the immune system to cure all types of disorders. I didn't realize that the senator and Jean Mechan only planned on selling it to the wealthy people who could afford the exorbitant price." He paused. "Jessie and I were the only team members who believed it should be available to all. The others weren't interested in a world cure, as a matter of fact, they were quite against it. The team disbanded when the senator and Dr. Mechan began a power struggle."

"Jessie and my mom were the test subjects?" Ada asked.

"Yes, but Simone was also heavily invested in Mechan's pharmaceutical company." He chuckled, "she was always in the lab looking over shoulders, a real quick study actually. The last time I saw your mother she was on her way to Paris to marry Jean Mechan. She disappeared a year later."

"So that Mechan guy was the last person to see her before she disappeared?" Ada asked while staring at the picture.

"Yes, but Mechan looked everywhere for her. He wanted that vaccine as much for himself as the money it would make him. He even had a man watch my home for over a month, suspicious that I might be hiding her. My guess is she found out about Mechan's taste for the ladies. Your mother wasn't the type to suffer a womanizer, and like Jessie she was good at disappearing." The doorbell caused them to jump.

"That must be the pizza, come inside and we'll eat." He disappeared around the corner.

Ada stared at the photograph. It was hard to have feelings for a woman she had no memory of. She leafed through the rest of the file. There were more photos some with Mechan the others with strangers. The last photo was of Simone and Jessie talking. It didn't look like a friendly conversation. The only other thing was an index card marked forwarding address: Jean Michel Mechan, 64 Rue Bavure, Paris, France.

"Pizza's going to get cold," Jessie said poking her head around the corner.

Ada followed her into the kitchen and sat down at a table with two large pizzas and a smiling professor. She listened to the conversation on the scientific discoveries the professor had made while she picked at her food.

"Did anyone even bother looking for my mother?"

Ada interrupted. They both stared at her a moment before answering.

"Like I said, I think she got tired of Mechan's womanizing," the professor said defensively. "I knew of her disappearance only through Jessie."

"As long as I've known your mother, she's always come and gone as she pleased. We received a large sum of money for participating in the testing. I finished the senator's battery of tests. Your mother left with Mechan and didn't allow any further testing to be done on her, and from the phone arguments I heard between the senator and Mechan, she kept all of the money."

"But, did you ever try to find her?" Ada asked staring directly at Jessie.

"No, I was busy with other things," she answered abruptly. "Mechan accused me of knowing where she was and then I went into hiding and have heard nothing since. She could be back with him for all I know."

Ada sat silently while they continued their conversation about the professor's theories on the healing process.

How could they want to help total strangers and just turn their backs on a friend? Was her mother trapped in a foreign land hoping someone cared enough to look? Ada remembered when she had fallen asleep in the graveyard and Dave and Carla hadn't even noticed she was gone. She had awoken in complete darkness.

Clouds and trees prevented the moonlight from

guiding her out, so she couldn't leave until the first morning light. Jessie and the professor were treating Simone with the same disregard. Listening to them talk made Ada angrier. Rain pelting the bay window reminded her of the quiet corner on the wrap-a-round porch, so she stood to go out.

"Ada, I wanted to ask you something," the professor said, turning his full attention toward her.

She plopped back into the chair with a quiet sigh.

"I received a phone call yesterday morning from Joseph. He's the man who..."

"I remember him," Ada interrupted.

Professor Strathern took on a more serious posture and expression.

"The paraplegic boy is walking." He stared at her as if anticipating a reaction.

Ada shrugged, "good for him."

"I don't think you realize how amazing this is." He gave Jessie a puzzled look, but she just leaned back in her seat and remained silent.

"This level of healing surpasses anything we've seen before. Not to undermine Jessie's ability, but if the disease or injury is past a certain point, she can't stimulate their system enough to heal. What you've done with this boy," he stopped and stared at her, "changes everything."

"So, what's the question?" Ada asked, her face expressionless.

"If we could run some tests, we could..."

"Forget it, I'm not a guinea pig and I'm not doing any of your stupid tests. I've heard this crap before." She looked straight at Jessie. "Sickness is here for a reason, no matter how bad it sucks. I won't help you change the world into standing room only."

"Your concern is legitimate Ada, but quality would eventually balance out quantity," the professor said, looking to Jessie again for support. "I believe people would implement and accept new laws on population control in order to be assured a full life free of sickness."

"I suppose we won't need jails or police anymore because people will just suddenly want to follow all the rules. And let me guess people like Senator Grimes are going to be the ones making the new rules," Ada said raising her voice so he couldn't interrupt. "How about this professor, you come up with a shot that actually makes people give a shit about something besides themselves and we'll talk tests, until then sickness and death are the only things that halfway keep people in line." She let the porch door slam behind her.

The cold, moist night air cooled her temper. She sat in the corner annoyed that Jessie thought it was so important to help strangers and so easy to forget her mother.

"For the first time I understand why some things should be forced in order to help humanity as a whole," Jessie said stepping forward from the darkness.

"Well then, maybe you'll get caught and forced by the right people, whoever they are." Ada brushed past her and went inside to ask the professor which room she was sleeping in.

He showed her to an upstairs room and leaned against the door frame as if he had something to say, but Ada busied herself with fitting the pictures and address of her mother into the front pocket of her backpack. When she turned around, he was gone.

After cleaning herself up she sat by the window staring into the wet darkness. Her light was off so she could see shadowy outlines in the yard and the illuminated falling rain directly under the street lights.

The clock read three in the morning when Ada decided to leave. There was no reason to continue on with Jessie. They had such different ideas on life. Besides, it was time to find her mother and figure out whether she was missing or hiding.

Everyone was asleep but Ada didn't want to take any chances on waking them and being stopped. She put on her backpack and slid the window open quietly. It was still pouring when she stepped out onto the rooftop. She closed the window to the warm room. The rain was already soaking into her, so she pulled up the hood of her sweatshirt and sat on the edge of the roof. She scooted and then dropped off the side not noticing a rhododendron bush below. The snapping rattle of the bush made her jump to her feet.

She found the path in the back of the house and followed it around to the front gate.

The streets were empty except for millions of drops of falling water.

She turned to see the house and noticed the long silhouette of Professor Strathern from behind the stained glass window, watching her.

She quickly disappeared into the darkness.

8

Walking usually cleared Ada's mind, but by seven in the morning she was cold, drenched and exhausted. She had stopped at several broken down motels but none would accept her money without photo ID. Her birth certificate wasn't good enough. In order to find her mother she was going to need a credit card and a passport, but most importantly, sleep. Wet park benches were starting to look like the only option.

She came to a residential area just outside of the city. The pouring rain cleared the streets of people and animals. An open window in a large brick church caught her attention. The window was level to the ground and was propped open with a broom stick handle that had been cut down to size. Ada peeked into a large meticulously clean kitchen.

Once inside she locked the window and laid the broomstick on the windowsill. She used her sleeve to wipe her muddy footprints off of the white counter. Her squeaking high tops echoed through the silent church, so she took them off and carried them. At one end of the kitchen was a door that led back outside; at the other end were two double doors that opened into a small cafeteria packed with folded up tables and chairs. She walked softly through the dining area to another set of double doors. These opened to a sanctuary lined with empty wooden pews all facing in the direction of a podium with a large wooden cross hanging behind it. The dim light made her feel like she was sleep walking, and so far every room was too open for her to sleep. The smell of old books and freshly polished wood reminded her of a library. She turned to go back to the dining room and noticed a circular staircase tucked in the corner and tiptoed up to have a look.

At the top of the stairs she carefully pushed open a hatch that opened into a bell tower. She climbed in and closed the hatch behind her.

There were four open arches protected by screens that allowed a cold breeze to blow through the room. A bell hung above Ada's head just out of reach. A long, thick rope with a wooden handle stretched from the bell to the floor. She laughed to herself at the thought of the chaos that would occur if she gave the rope a good hard pull. There was a cupboard that ran the length of a wall that overlooked a parking lot and garden; it seemed like a perfect fit. She pushed a few dusty books and a bottle of wood polish to the back and crawled inside. As quickly as she closed the cupboard door she fell asleep.

It was late afternoon when Ada finally awoke and came quietly down the stairs of the bell tower into the empty church.

She helped herself to a peanut butter sandwich from the kitchen and found a phone and phone book in a corner of the dining room. It was time to get a credit card and passport. She picked a bank from the address book, wrote down a list of questions, dialed the phone and was put on hold. After an annoying one way conversation with an electronic voice, she finally spoke to a person who rambled off a list of what she would need to do in order to receive a debit card that directly withdrew from her bank account. The PIN number Jessie gave her acted as an ID over the phone, but to get money Ada needed a debit card. The banks were located in Switzerland and New York, so going to pick the card up was impossible. She had to have an address that the bank could send the card to, and the church seemed to be her only option.

She tried not to sound surprised when the lady said the amount in the account was over a million dollars. Even when Ada did have a little cash she was never in a big hurry to spend it, but this wiped away all money worries. She told the bank lady she would call back shortly with an address.

She hung up the phone feeling a bit guilty, after all, Jessie was looking out for her. They just didn't see eye to eye on a healer's obligation. As soon as she found an internet connection she would drop Jessie an email, to let her know she was okay.

Ada ran up and grabbed her backpack just in case she got locked out. The bell tower was the perfect place to hang low and wait for the debit card. If the church had a mailbox she could figure out when the postman came and be the first person to get the mail. All she had to do was find the address.

She went out the kitchen window, making sure it was unlocked, then headed to the front of the church where most addresses and mailboxes were located, but all she found was a small cottage that looked like a miniature version of the church with "office" written above the door. Her heart sank when she noticed an address running along the side of the door and a mailbox on the other side. Someone passed in front of the window, so she stepped out of view.

She needed an address. All she could think of was renting a P.O. Box or finding an abandoned building. She followed a garden path up to double doors in a glass lobby and pressed her forehead against the glass. It looked like it opened up into the sanctuary just underneath the bell tower. She tried to open the doors but they were locked. Taped to the window next to the door were flyers stating times for different meetings. Ada stepped back to have a better look and noticed a mail slot built into the bottom of the door. There had to be an address. She checked along the sides of the porch and found, hidden by some overgrown bushes, the numbers. She got a pen from her backpack and wrote the address in the leather book.

"It's nice to see one of our youth so interested in church." Ada spun around to find a priest standing on the path smiling. "I didn't mean to startle you. May I help? You seem like you're looking for something." She remembered one of the gatherings on the flyer in the window.

"Girl Scouts," she blurted. "I'm looking for information on Girl Scouts."

"We certainly can help you with that." He rested his hand gently on her shoulder. "Come right in and we'll get you the contact information you need." He turned her in the direction of the office. "My name is Father John. Who might you be?"

"Uh, Alice." She went along quietly so she wouldn't look suspicious.

The office had the same type of highly polished furniture as the church, but mixed with the sweet wood smell was the thick, musty smell of an old shag carpet that felt damp under foot.

"Janis, we have a young lady out here in need of Girl Scout information." After a few moments of rustling and creaking an old woman hobbled into the room. Her shoulders and back were twisted and curved and a large growth on the nape of her neck caused her chin to stay locked to her chest. Ada could feel the exhausted confusion of the woman's body trying to battle the affliction. Many times Ada had been reprimanded for staring, but such extreme illness held her attention forcing her to try and solve the body's mysterious reaction.

"Janis has been working here for over twenty years.

She's one of our oldest employees and parishioners." Father John seemed to be addressing Ada's staring.

Janis acknowledged Ada by lifting her eyes to the side. She reached the desk and started rifling through a stack of papers. Ada noticed her fingers were as bent and rounded as her back with large bulging bumps at each joint. Janis carefully put the information in a small white envelope and held it out for her to take. Ada tried to ignore the sickness, but she already knew what Janis's body needed to do to fix it. It was like staring at words and trying not to read them. Ada took the envelope and quickly turned to leave.

"They meet in the dining hall at seven if you want to get started tonight," Janis said.

"Thanks," Ada said over her shoulder as she closed the door behind her.

She walked along the sidewalk, so she could see the name of the street, the last piece of information to solve the bank problem. She felt the pressure of their eyes watching her as she disappeared around the corner.

The bank would have to wait until tomorrow. She didn't want to end up caught if they suspected something and came snooping around. She quickly disappeared up the spiral staircase and settled into her cupboard and listened to music until she finally dozed off.

Ada got started early the next morning with the bank. She was disappointed to find that it would take five to seven business days before her debit card would come.

Ordering her passport and buying the plane ticket would have to wait until the card came.

By the first evening she was bored and tired of the darkness. Besides the cupboard, the safest but creepiest place to use her flashlight was the church basement where she found a shower to wash and do laundry. A schedule for gatherings was hung in the hallway outside the sanctuary, so Ada knew afternoons needed to be spent outside of the church. A library several blocks away kept her busy researching her travel plans and studying French. During the early morning she tracked the postal person. She realized she needed to figure out the exact time of delivery.

Each day, at around nine in the morning, a different carrier delivered mail to the office but not the church, so she decided to clear away the branches hiding the church's address hoping the carrier would follow the address listed on the envelope instead of taking everything to the office.

On the seventh day Ada was startled to see a break in the routine. She watched from the doorway of the sanctuary as the mailman stopped at the mouth of the path, re-read the letter he had in his hand, looked at the numbers running along the side of the church door and then slowly walked up the path slipping an envelope into the slot on the door. Ada could barely wait for him to disappear down the sidewalk when she crept out and grabbed the envelope. She saw her name and tucked it in her back pocket, grabbed her backpack and headed to the library before the church meetings started up.

On the way she stopped at a bench in front of a park and opened the envelope pulling out a shiny black plastic card with her name and a string of numbers embossed on it. She found a cash machine in front of a bank and swiped it through, then typed in the PIN from her book, answered an array of questions and out came two hundred dollars. She looked around to make sure no one was watching.

Ada smiled each time she came across a cash machine, but she quickly learned when trying to build up some cash that two hundred dollars was all it would give her a day. Her passport was a much bigger hassle.

At the library, she was able to print off the paperwork, but finding a place that made passport photos meant a bus ride to a shop that specialized in that kind of thing.

After getting everything together and paying to have her passport rushed, Ada still had to wait two weeks for it. Boredom was starting to make her reckless. She left her own groceries in the refrigerator and laid her clothes to dry on top of the cupboard in the bell tower.

Early in the morning, a week into her wait for the passport, she heard voices close to the bell tower hatch. She opened the cupboard and quickly pulled in her clothes. The voice of Father John and another man emerged into the tower. The hatch slammed closed and footsteps moved just outside the cupboard doors.

PASSPORT

"There isn't too much in need of cleaning up here. We'll focus most of the effort on the kitchen and the windows."

"We have well over seventy volunteers this year, quite a turn out." Father John's voice sounded proud.

"It looks like someone has already started the dusting process up here." Ada heard what sounded like a hand brush over the top of the cupboard. A momentary silence made her expect the cupboard door to fly open at any second.

"This room gets little use; we'll just let it be. After you Mr. Decker." She heard the hatch close softly.

It was over an hour before she had the nerve to come out. She expected to see the priest sitting quietly outside when she opened the cupboard, but the bell tower was conveniently empty.

The spring cleaning didn't start until afternoon, so she was able to keep track of the postal carriers. Three days before the delivery date the tall bearded mailman, who always lingered longer in the office than the others, stopped in front of the sanctuary path and looked back and forth between the front of the lobby and a brown colored envelope he held in his hand. With a confused expression he shook his head and started for the office.

Ada sprung for the door to catch him but it was locked. It would be easier dealing with the postman than going back in the office. She raced around the building, but by the time she made it to the front of the church he was already closing the office door behind him. She glared at him as he passed. He gave her a puzzled look in return. She rested her hand on the doorknob trying to come up with a plausible excuse. There was none.

She opened the door slowly poking her head in first. Janis was seated at her desk going through a small pile of mail. Ada saw the side of the brown envelope poking out of the pile.

"Hello Janis, I don't know if you remember, but I was here a few weeks ago." She paused while Janis turned sideways to look at her out of the corner of her eye.

"The young lady interested in Girl Scouts," she answered quickly. "Did you sign up?"

"Huh? Oh, no I actually have a small problem," Ada stumbled surprised that she had remembered her.

Janis gave a sympathetic look. "I'm sorry Father John isn't going to be in this afternoon. You can come first thing in the morning. We can set up an appointment." Janis said opening a daily planner.

Ada knew Father John would have too many questions, and she wanted to be on her way.

"That envelope is for me. I had to have it sent here because I have nowhere else I can trust. It has my passport and birth certificate in it. You can even check." She waited as Janis picked up the envelope and stared at it bewildered.

Janis read the front of it, "Ada Elisabeth Larue. Is that you?" She asked while grabbing a letter opener and carefully sliding it across the top of the envelope. The large knots on her joints made the smallest movement awkward. Ada leaned forward to see the little, blue book that would allow her to travel. Janis looked at the passport picture and then turned sideways to see Ada's face.

"I'm sorry to bother you like this, but I needed a safe address," Ada said.

"Is your home life so bad you can't receive mail?" Janis asked putting the passport and birth certificate back in the envelope and resting her hand on it.

"I'm trying to find my mother." The truth sounded so strange.

"Oh my, really this is something you should discuss with Father John. He's a good man and he'll help."

Ada's heart sank. Father John would want to contact her legal guardian, and then she would end up back with Gretchen or worse. Janis stood and made her way around the desk to Ada.

"Passports and Birth Certificates are very serious legal documents. You really need to keep these safe." She gently grabbed Ada's hand and put the envelope in it, "I really hope you come tomorrow and talk to Father John."

Ada was stunned that her passport was actually in her hand. She was ready to get started on the next step of her journey. Janis smiled watching from the corner of her eye; chin still firmly fixed to her chest.

"Janis, will you hold my hands?" Ada folded and slipped the envelope into her back pocket.

"Do you need a prayer?" Janis asked surprised.

"Uh...yeah. Sure." Ada grabbed Janis's hands and held them firmly. She felt the burning and tingling, but this time in her mind she could see the chaos in Janis's system and exactly how to repair the damage. She let the heat flow with more control, focusing and directing it. Janis absorbed the heat as fast as Ada released it melting away the build up around her joints, until a loud sob jolted Ada back to attention.

"Good God child!" Janis lifted her head and looked straight at Ada. "How is this possible?"

Ada let go of her hands. They were smooth, free of knots.

Janis reached for her, "No, don't leave, please wait." But Ada was already out the door.

It was definitely time to go.

She raced to the church window and ran up the circular stairs to grab her belongings from the cupboard, and then straight out the back door making sure no one was following her.

Ada caught a bus to Portland Airport. Her stomach turned as she walked past the backed up cars three lanes across with people rushing in every direction loaded with suitcases. The inside of the terminal was worse. Everywhere Ada turned people were standing in lines with stacks of luggage. Returning to the quiet darkness of the church was tempting, but she wanted to find her mother.

She found an area with Wi-Fi and looked up flights to Paris. One left at 11pm that evening. She bought a ticket at an automated kiosk near a ticketing counter that checked her in and spit out a boarding pass. If only security could be this easy she thought, grabbing her pass.

Ada maneuvered through the crowd until she came to the long snaking lines that led up to security. People were being forced to open bags and remove shoes. Guards were trained to notice odd situations. Too many questions and she might screw up. She looked around for a family to try and stick close to, but instead a juice bar caught her eye. She left the line and went to purchase a large fruit smoothie.

By the time she made it to the front of security her smoothie had turned to warm compote. She watched her backpack disappear into the x-ray machine.

"Where are your parents?" the security guard asked, before she stepped through the metal detector.

"They're already at the gate. They said I had plenty of time to get one of these." She held up her juice smoothie and smiled. He waved her through.

She grabbed her pack trying not to look too anxious when she remembered she forgot to take out her mini sewing scissors she'd bought at the secondhand store. Signs everywhere warned not to bring sharp items on the planes. She looked over her shoulder to make sure they weren't running after her. Anymore stupid mistakes like that and she might as well call Gretchen herself she thought as she cut across the flow of people to a bathroom and tossed the smoothie into the trash.

After splashing cold water on her face and putting her hair in a ponytail, Ada went to find the gate where the plane would depart from.

The boarding area was empty except for a man stretched across several chairs sleeping. Ada pulled off her backpack and plopped into a chair. She still had seven hours until her plane departed so she bought a book to study more French from a shop across the walkway and settled in for a long wait.

By evening the chairs around Ada were filling quickly. She watched frantic people race to their gates from over the top of her book. An old woman situated herself in the seat directly across from her. She kept squinting at Ada and then fished a cloth from her purse and carefully cleaned her glasses. Ada tried to look busy with her book.

"You're studying French?" the old woman asked with a heavy accent.

"Trying."

"Because you are on this flight?" the woman pointed to Ada's gate.

"Yep," she put her nose deeper in her book.

"Where are your parents?" the woman asked concerned.

Ada looked at the stewardesses by the gate hoping they weren't listening.

"I'm meeting my mom in Paris."

"You must be nervous travelling alone. You're so young." She pulled a small suitcase and her purse over to the seat next to Ada and sat down, "I'm flying alone too. You know, I can help you with that." She nodded at Ada's book. "My name is Madame Jardin," she held out her hand.

"I'm Ada." She quickly shook hands trying to ignore the severe imbalance in Madame Jardin's blood. "Pronunciation is the most important thing," Madame Jardin said taking the book from Ada's hand.

They worked for over an hour on correct pronunciation. Madame Jardin made her repeat words until finally she would pat Ada's leg and say "parfait." Then she decided, for more study time, they needed to sit next to each other on the plane. She went to the small ticket desk in front of the gate and confused the flight attendants so badly that by the end Madame Jardin and Ada had seats next to each other, which made boarding the plane smooth and question free.

They had three seats near a window all to themselves. Ada leaned back hardly noticing the take off. The constant hum of Madame Jardin's voice had a relaxing effect on her, but randomly Madame Jardin would stop talking and nod off.

The dinner cart rattled to a stop next to them. Ada watched the stewardess pull a special plate from a drawer in the bottom of the cart while Madame Jardin explained that she couldn't take all of the sugar in the regular meals, but Madame Jardin's salmon dinner looked far tastier than the wormy spaghetti Ada tried to choke down.

After the lights dimmed and everyone settled down to sleep Ada decided to work on exercising her new skill. She fished the sewing scissors from her backpack and turned toward the window. A movie had just started on the screen that was embedded in the headrest in front of her. She rested her left hand flat on the corner of her fold out dinner tray. Across the back of her hand, she pressed the point of one of the scissors' blades into her skin and began dragging it from one side to the other. The first two tries only made thin, chalky, useless scratches, so she clenched her teeth and squinted, putting her weight into it. A deep slice followed the point of the scissors. It quickly filled with blood that in some spots spilled over, streaking her hand.

Ada continued with the cut, ignoring the stinging and burning, until the bloody slice stretched to her arm. She sat for a moment watching little streams of blood join up with bigger ones that dripped onto the foldout tray. Her mind already had a picture of the cells rebuilding the cut. It was interesting that it remained only a picture unless she directed the energy to it. She focused her thoughts on the cells rebuilding. The slice smoothed and closed until all that was left were the streams of blood on her hand and three little pools on the tray. She pulled her sleeve down to wipe away the blood. Her goal was to speed up the healing process.

It took several cuts, but she realized the pain took her mind away from being able to heal quickly, and the quicker she could heal the less pain there would be. With this new understanding, she practiced ignoring the pain and training her mind to focus on healing.

The movie credits were rolling down the screen when she finally accomplished what she wanted. As she dragged the scissors across her hand the cut disappeared directly behind the point only allowing tiny beads of blood to sporadically appear. The wrinkled hand of Madame Jardin gently covered the top of Ada's.

"I'm not sure how you're doing that, but you don't want to frighten people in such a confined space," she whispered in Ada's ear.

Ada quickly wiped the rest of the blood away and shoved the sewing scissors into her backpack. She wasn't sure if Madame Jardin really understood what was going on, so she picked up the French book and started reading as if nothing had happened.

Ada spent the rest of the flight studying and listening to Madame Jardin talk about her childhood in Paris and how things have changed. Before she knew it, a bell was drawing her attention to a locking seatbelt sign.

Ada looked out the window to see the city below getting closer. She hadn't given any real thought to what she would do when she arrived in Paris. Dealing with French customs might not be so easy. She pressed her forehead against the window pretending to be interested in the landing while trying to think of a plan.

By the time they bounced onto the runway all Ada had come up with was to use Jean Mechan's address as the place she would be staying. She was hoping it would be like customs in Canada, quick and few questions.

The plane was empty by the time Madame Jardin had tidied up and gathered her things. Ada carried Madame Jardin's suitcase, while Madame Jardin searched her purse for her passport. The gate area was empty except for a few straggling passengers hugging and chatting with relatives or friends.

"Shouldn't your mother be here to pick you up?" Madame Jardin asked looking around as Ada handed her the bag.

"There's something I want to help you with," Ada said. Even though they'd only known each other for a few hours, it seemed like Madame Jardin had been a friend for much longer, and Ada could see her sickness was only going to get worse.

"Oh no my dear, it's you I'm worried about," she interrupted. "Where is your mother?"

She steered Ada off to the side where no one could hear them talk. "Is your mother in France?"

Ada dropped down in one of the interlinked airport seats. When Madame Jardin took a seat next to her she unloaded bits and pieces of what had happened to her since she had decided to voice her protests on Carla and Dave's living room wall. Telling her story clarified the risk she was taking coming to France alone, but it was also a relief to say out loud the reality that felt like a weird dream. She skimmed over the extent of her healing ability and the trouble with the senator and his thugs. Madame Jardin listened quietly, occasionally resting her hand on Ada's knee.

"You're young for such troubles," she said shaking her head. "I have two rooms in my apartment that I don't use. I would like it if you would stay in one of them. It's not far from the street you're looking for and it will give you time to think things through." She stood letting Ada know she wouldn't take no for an answer.

"We need to get our baggage now, or they might give them to someone else."

"This is all I have," Ada said standing up and sliding her backpack on.

All the way to baggage claim Madame Jardin talked of how amazing it was that a girl Ada's age carried so few belongings and started naming all of the items that a seventy-five-year old woman has to bring even for a short trip.

Ada was quiet most of the taxi ride to the apartment taking in all of the new scenery. Signs and advertisements in French made her realize how far from home she was. The buildings were antique and ornate compared to what she was used to in Seattle. Statues overlooked the city from building tops and corners, and fountains took the place of traffic lights at four way intersections.

Madame Jardin had thoroughly described the area she'd lived her entire life, so when they passed the little fold out souvenir stalls along the river's edge Ada knew they were close. After a few blocks they pulled up in front of a five story apartment building surrounded by a stone and wrought iron fence. Ada wondered if the people inside dressed as fancy as the building they lived in. She reached in her backpack for money to pay the taxi fare and realized the money would be different as well. Madame Jardin laughed and motioned Ada to put it away.

"I'm used to taxis. I've never had a car. If I did I certainly wouldn't know how to drive it."

Madame Jardin put her suitcase and bag in a small closet size elevator and sent it to the top floor while they took the stairs. She gave Ada a step by step tour of the building that five generations of Jardins had called home. The inside of the building had rich décor like the outside but was far more tattered and worn. Every floor they passed Madame Jardin named the owner of each apartment, and told something personal about their lives or appearances. She started trying to say everything in French, and only used English if Ada gave her a puzzled look.

At the top floor Ada pulled the luggage from the elevator and rolled it into the apartment. A long hall led into a living room where Madame Jardin stopped in front of an oversized window that pulled open.

"Come and look," she said. At first Ada didn't notice the tip of the large black steeple that poked just above the rooftops, but on careful direction from Madame Jardin she found it.

"Notre Dame Cathedral," she smiled and was surprised when Ada didn't recognize the name. The endless stretch of rooftops was more interesting to her than a lone steeple.

The apartment was spacious with tall ceilings and lots of windows, unusually quiet considering the busy city just outside, but Ada's favorite place was the balcony. Part of it was covered while the other half was open to the city. Plants were everywhere tangling up and down trellises and overflowing from pots on the ground. A wooden table and chairs trimmed with lacy carvings were the only pieces of furniture.

It would be a perfect place to sit back and listen to the rumble of the city or pull a chair up to the railing and watch the people and cars weave down the narrow streets. The building across was like a wall of TVs with all of the windows that looked right into people's lives.

Ada settled in to watch when Madame Jardin asked her to pick a bedroom, so she followed her back into the apartment. One room was next to Madame Jardin's and the other was a small loft with a circular staircase leading up to it. Ada chose the loft because it reminded her of the quiet solitude of the bell tower. She tucked her backpack under the bed and lay back for a moment to think about the last twenty-four hours. It was hard to believe she was actually in France. With Madame Jardin, it didn't feel like a foreign country at all.

Ada went back down to the balcony and stared out at the endless stretch of buildings wondering if her mom even wanted to be found.

9

Madame Jardin included Ada into her routine as if she'd always been a part of it. Mornings began with breakfast on the balcony consisting of a foul smelling cheese that Ada decided tasted a little better than it smelled, a cup of fruit that according to Madame Jardin helped the cheese back out, and a long stick of bread that was purchased at a corner bakery, which was the first of Ada's errands.

Food had to be fresh and everything seemed to have its own specialty market, so she would make the rounds picking up foods at the neighborhood shops, and it was the only way Madame Jardin would let her help.

Ada bought a map of Paris at the corner bookstore. When Madame Jardin discovered her looking at it in the living room, she set up tea and small cakes on the balcony and spread the map out on the table. It was like watching someone open a long lost photo album. She used a pencil to mark the safest and quickest way. Ada sat quietly watching and nodding as Madame Jardin explained the notable places on the map and the dangerous areas to avoid. Few people had shown her such concern.

When she found her mother, would she have to leave Madame Jardin? Ada couldn't help thinking again that her mother might not want to see her; maybe she had a new family, or didn't want to be reminded of the past.

She folded the map and slipped it into the front pocket of her backpack. When things slowed down she would plan a visit to her mother's; until then, she would enjoy the time she had with Madame Jardin.

Visits to and from neighbors took up the afternoons. Ada usually listened quietly during these meetings hoping not to be included, but Monsieur Reneau, an older man sharing the same floor with Madame Jardin, always needed to question Ada about the younger generation's complete disregard for tradition and good moral value. Ada was still working on her French, so she couldn't say all she wanted to, but only shrugged her shoulders and made a few simple comments.

Two weeks had passed before Ada went out to look around on her own without a list of groceries to pick up. She took the map, so she could at least pass by her mother's apartment, and see what it looked like. She started out along the river, but it was crowded with people browsing the souvenir stalls, so she made her way to a residential area plotting each block on the map.

She heard the whine of a moped coming behind her and turned just in time to see a large truck change lanes, and hit the moped, sending it and the rider spinning out of control. Ada winced as the rider slammed against one of the trees that lined the street. She watched the truck drive away either intentionally or unaware.

Two men raced toward the rider, who ended up being a young woman. By the way they kept kneeling next to the woman and then standing and yelling frantically for help, Ada knew she was badly hurt. Part of her wanted to walk past and forget what she saw, but the other part wanted to see how bad the injuries were, and if she could heal them quickly or even at all.

She slowly approached the scene. The men were speaking French so fast it was difficult to understand what they were saying. She edged closer when one ran to the corner for help. The other noticed her and asked about a cell phone. She shook her head no. When he stood and went to the curb to flag cars on the street for help, Ada knelt down to look at the girl. Her head had taken the full force of the blow against the tree. She was out cold and had a large gash that ran from the top of her forehead to the middle of her cheek, but Ada understood her internal injuries were much worse.

Swelling around her brain was starting to put pressure on blood flow, and a broken rib had damaged her left lung. Ada laid her hands on the girl's chest and focused. The gushing head wound was the first to disappear. She felt the energy level slightly change when the internal injuries were completely healed. As soon as the girl's eyes opened, Ada stood up and came face to face with the man who had been flagging people on the curb.

"What did you do?" he gasped looking from Ada to the confused girl on the ground who was now sitting up. She understood his French completely but just shrugged her shoulders as if she didn't, and quickly walked away looking back to make sure she wasn't being followed. Her mother's apartment would have to wait. She stopped for bread and cheese and then headed back to Madame Jardin's.

"There you are," Madame Jardin said meeting Ada at the opening to the living room. "I have something I want to give you." With trembling hands she handed Ada a tattered book with yellowed pages.

"It was my favorite book when I was a young girl. I will teach you to read it."

Ada quickly set down the bread and cheese, wiped her hands on her pants, and took the book.

"Thank you," she smiled, but she could feel Madame Jardin needed one of her shots. The last time Ada tried to mention the illness, Madame Jardin refused to discuss it and sent Ada on an errand to the post office to drop off letters.

"I know you don't believe me, but I can really help you with this."

Madame Jardin smiled, "diabetes is complicated, but thank you for your concern."

"That's true, but it won't make it worse if I try."

Madame Jardin sat down on the couch with a skeptical look. Ada rested her hands on Madame Jardin's shoulders and within a few seconds pulled away. The trembling was gone and the beads of sweat were already drying up on her forehead. She sat staring at Ada with a bewildered look and then hurried to her room returning with the machine that checked her blood.

She pricked her finger, wiped it on a thin white strip and then inserted it into the device. She stared at the screen for a moment puzzled and then repeated the whole process again.

"Before you came it said I needed my shot, and I felt like I needed my shot." She shook her head. "Now it says I'm fine."

"Are you alright?" Ada asked worried about Madame Jardin's shocked expression.

"I've lived with diabetes for the last ten years of my life. I'm not sure what to feel, but I do feel so much better."

"Good," Ada said walking out to the balcony, "because you're kinda freaking me out."

She heard Madame Jardin setting the table behind her.

"Come sit down and have something to eat," she said smiling at Ada as she filled her plate. "This is a blessing from God, my dear. You have the healing touch."

"Where does blessing come into it?" Ada snapped feeling the heat rise in her cheeks, "God plagues humanity with who knows how many diseases, and then blesses a couple people with the ability to heal. Sounds more like a fluke to me, or maybe a God with a mean sense of humor."

Nothing was said the rest of the meal. Ada wanted to change the subject to one of the usual topics, but found Madame Jardin's unusual silence too frustrating.

"I'm going to check out Bavure Street. I'll stop by the markets on my way back." She grabbed her dishes and turned to go to the kitchen.

Madame Jardin gently rested her hand on Ada's forearm. "Sometimes there are no explanations for why things are the way they are. We just accept them as miracles."

"I'm sorry I snapped at you," Ada said as she sat down. "It's just there are all these crappy things going on in the world, and a few good things happen and God gets all the credit for blessing people. If that's the case then why doesn't He just stop all the crap?"

"I try not to think of things like this, but I believe humans can only appreciate the good things if they come through hardship; otherwise we just seem to take comforts and contented times for granted."

Chiming church bells overpowered the endless rumble and honking of the streets below. Ada was relieved to step into the flow of people on the busy sidewalk. She'd healed Madame Jardin and then managed to depress her. Time away would probably do them both good.

It took almost an hour to get to the street.

The apartment was in a well kept area with less traffic. The building stood ten stories high with gargoyles on each corner, craning their necks as if keeping an eye on the passing people below.

She tried to walk in through the front doors, but a grumpy doorman quickly cut her off, ignoring all of her questions before sending her on her way. She knew her French was clear enough; he either didn't want to be bothered or he'd never heard of Jean Mechan or Simone Larue.

It took two hours of waiting and watching, but finally a delivery truck pulled up at the corner. While the doorman was helping unload a few pieces of furniture Ada slipped past. She took the elevator, checking each floor for the apartment number, but nothing matched. It had to be the top floor marked "penthouse," when she pressed the elevator button it beeped for a code. She punched in a few combinations resulting in an obnoxious buzz.

She got out on the ninth floor and tried the stairwell but the door was locked. An open window at the end of the hall caught her attention.

She looked down at the sidewalk below. It wasn't that high up, not anything like the bridge in Canada. She looked up and could see a silky crimson curtain rippling on the wind out of the penthouse window. Ada leaned out to see how close it was. If she stretched, it seemed like she could reach it. She put her knee on the window sill, held the inside wall and used her other hand to feel for the ledge above. The old spinning nauseous feeling came back with a vengeance, so she lowered herself back in and rested her forehead against the wall.

"You've got to be kidding," she grumbled aloud planting her foot firmly on the window sill. She angrily thrust upward slamming her head on the top of the window frame.

After steadying herself, she hooked her arm on the inside wall and tried again. The curtain was just out of reach, taunting her. There was no way a fear of heights was going to stop her. She pushed up on the tips of her toes and felt the curtain brush her fingertips, only a little further she thought. She leaned out and stretched as far as she could without looking down. Her fingers had just bumped the underside of the ledge when the mumble of voices drifted down from above. She tried to duck quickly back in, but lost her footing and fell inside slamming her ribs against the window sill on the way in.

Even though her injuries healed fast, there was always that split second of excruciating pain. It wouldn't be long before someone came to investigate, so she snuck back down the stairwell, found the emergency exit, and slipped out with a stinging alarm sounding behind her.

It was dusk before Ada made her way back to Madame Jardin's. She still wasn't sure how she would get up to the penthouse, but staking out the building was the plan for tomorrow.

She stepped into the apartment to find Madame Jardin sitting in the front room with Madame Julienne from the second floor. Madame Jardin stood quickly and pulled Ada back into the hallway, speaking to her surprisingly in English.

"I don't want to put you on the spot, but Isabel is in such pain. Her bones give her so much trouble." She pulled Ada closer whispering directly into her ear. "Three months ago she bent down to tie her shoe and broke her back in two places. If you could just help her like you helped me. I've explained to her that she can't tell another soul," she smiled pleadingly.

Ada had already sensed Madame Julienne's bone problems, but sudden healing miracles would draw attention, and people like the senator were waiting for any clue to catch a healer. Ada took a step back, but Madame Jardin's pleading look made her feel guilty.

"Make sure she doesn't tell anyone, even her doctor." Ada gave a frustrated look as she went in and sat down on the couch. She rested her hands on Madame Julienne's forearms. Her body soaked in Ada's energy rebuilding the brittle bones. Madame Julienne smiled broadly while talking non-stop through the whole process as if she could feel each bone reinforcing itself.

A few minutes later Ada went to sit out on the balcony leaving both ladies chattering happily about Madame Julienne gaining a couple inches of height. She left the lights off and watched the people in their illuminated apartments busily going about their lives.

Healing people in Madame Jardin's building seemed reckless, Ada thought looking down at the street below. It was unlikely that the senator could find her all the way in France, but she didn't want to take any chances. She would have to talk to Madame Jardin again about the danger of drawing too much attention because of miraculously cured diseases. A burst of laughter from the living room made her decide it could wait until morning.

After breakfast Ada ran all of her errands early, so she could spend the rest of the day staking out the penthouse. The front entrance had little action. She kept out of view in doorways across the street.

By noon only two people had left the building, the doorman, who had stood near the front door smoking a cigarette and a guy in a suit, who got into a fancy car and drove away. She decided to see if there was anything going on behind the building.

The only clear and unsuspicious view of the emergency exit was from the street corner at the opening of the alley. She sat down next to a lamp post and watched for another chance to sneak in, but all she ended up seeing was a black cat enjoying Parisian delicacies out of the community trash can.

Crashing metal mixed with laughter from an alley across the way sent the cat into hiding and brought Ada to her feet. The noise was certain to stir up the grumpy doorman, so she went to see what was going on.

A boy and a girl who looked around Ada's age were taking turns jumping off of the corner of a dumpster. Occasionally the boy would flip into a jump. The crashing sound happened when they pushed off too hard and the dumpster slammed against the brick wall behind.

While the girl was waiting for her turn to jump she would stare up at the top of the building. Ada followed her gaze and gasped. A dark haired boy was almost to the top, using the window ledges as his ladder. He pushed off of the bottom ledge to grasp the one above, then he would pull up and start again. His movements were so fast and smooth he might as well have been running up a flight of stairs. He came to the top window and disappeared onto the roof.

A moment later Ada watched in awe as he leapt to the building across the alley. The other boy was already halfway up the window ledge path while the girl used the dumpster to jump to a second floor fire escape. They climbed the building like a troop of monkeys climbing trees in the jungle. The girl was the last to leap over the alley from above and disappear into the labyrinth of rooftops.

Back home in Seattle, Ada had seen skateboarders and even break dancers doing crazy stunts on the streets, but nothing compared to what she had just seen.

She stepped back out onto the sidewalk and followed the trail of windows up to the flowing crimson curtain of the penthouse.

Locked doors and rude doormen wouldn't be a problem if she learned to climb buildings like they did.

Not to mention she could finally overcome her annoying fear of heights. It was time to learn to travel city streets the French way.

10

Ada stood in front of the penthouse apartment building and watched the doorman reading his paper. She had already circled a few surrounding blocks looking for the teenagers she had seen climbing the building the day before.

Madame Jardin had asked her to be back by four o'clock for a luncheon with Madame Cornot, one of the few people in the building Ada hadn't met. She hated being on a schedule, and she had a feeling there would be healing involved, but Madame Jardin seemed excited so she promised to be there. The day after healing Madame Julienne Ada explained to Madame Jardin that they had to be careful, miracles attracted attention, usually from the wrong people.

There was still no sign of the building jumping teenagers. The more she thought about them the more she realized it would be almost impossible to find them again. They could be running on the rooftops right above her and she'd never see them.

She still had four hours until the luncheon so she started walking further in the direction they'd disappeared.

Buildings changed from the fancy carved architecture to plain concrete block shapes. Graffiti took the place of statues and wrought iron. Artists in this part of the city were telling a different story.

She came upon a row of abandoned buildings with the first floor windows and doors cemented in with cinder blocks. A loud crash echoed from behind. She went around back to see if it was them. The same girl and boy who had been jumping from the dumpster were leaning against a cement divider watching the other boy jump from a second story window. As quickly as he landed on his feet he lunged into a roll making the two story drop look easy. He was tall with dark shoulder length hair. His strength and agility seemed to set him apart as the leader. The other two stood alert when he tried something different. Everything he came in contact with he seemed to use to propel himself forward. Unlike the others he was always in motion.

She thought she saw him glance at her from the corner of his eye when he passed to go to the next building. Even though the bottom window was cemented in, he ran right up it to the window above, and made his way to the roof the same as the day before. This time he crouched on the ledge waiting for the others to follow. Her heart started to race when she saw he was planning to jump to the next building. The gap seemed too wide. She considered turning away, but watched through squinted eyes. He came down with ease using the window ledges to grab and slow his fall.

“We don’t want a fan club, you know.” The girl was standing in front of Ada with crossed arms. She had blond hair cut just below her ears and a piercing above her eyebrow.

Ada stared in dismay. She understood most of the French, but the tone was unmistakable.

“Elaine, come on,” the other boy called. The dark haired one was already off in a different direction, so the others took off after him.

There was no way Ada could follow after such a stupid comment. She bit her lip and watched as they disappeared around the corner.

“Groupie. Wishful thinking,” Ada grumbled turning to the second story window they had been jumping from. “I can figure this out myself.”

Running up the wall was harder than he made it look. After ten exhausting attempts, she tried climbing up to the window by using the tiny ridges of the filled in bottom window. She slid down scraping her chin which healed as she walked back to make another run at it.

This time anger coupled with launching off a ridge helped her grab the ledge of the glassless window above. She hauled herself inside and fell in a crumpled heap on the dusty floor. Once she realized she could heal her tired trembling arms and legs she jumped to her feet and positioned herself in the window. Jumping out the window had to be easier.

It wasn’t that far of a drop she thought, trying to

calm her turning stomach. She leaned out to judge the distance to the ground.

"Keep your knees bent so you're ready for the landing." A voice said from behind causing her to almost slip out the window. She felt a hand grab the back of her shirt to steady her.

"You shouldn't sneak up on people," she grumbled stepping down out of the frame. She came face to face with the dark haired boy from the group.

"Huh?" he gave her a puzzled look.

She turned a violent shade of red and started over in French.

"Uh, okay, knees bent. Any other advice?" She felt her cheeks flush at how close he was standing to her. One step forward and she would be against his chest. He smiled making her whole face feel on fire. She turned and climbed back into the window frame. It wasn't the height causing her stomach to swirl this time.

"Practice on lower jumps." He grinned leaning against the wall. His arms were muscular from climbing. She could feel her own exhausted muscles trembling even with the constant healing.

Had he seen her struggle up the building and flop inside? She felt his dark eyes penetrating her profile. Standing this close to him made her heart pound. Before she had time to think it through, she jumped from the window.

The importance of crouching was evident when she hit the ground and felt her ankle fold under her. A loud snap accompanied by an excruciating stabbing pain made her fall backwards onto her butt. She grabbed the ankle and focused her attention on the torn tendon instead of the pain.

"Are you alright?" He was next to her looking for the injury. "You came down on your ankle."

"Nope, I'm good," she said standing and brushing herself off. "But I probably should try those lower jumps."

He gave her another amused grin. She felt the burning come back to her cheeks and looked at her feet. Guys didn't usually have this affect on her; it was annoying.

"Can you teach me how to run like you do?" she said trying to look as confident as she could. Unfortunately flushed cheeks and lumps in the throat weren't ailments she could heal. He was a few inches taller than her and considerably broader. Fighting the desire to look away she stood straight and faced the awkward silence with a determined stare.

"What's your name?" he asked.

"Ada."

"Why do you want to run, Ada?" The grin replaced by a serious expression.

"I..." she paused. "It seems like a good thing to know how to do."

The grin came back.

"Well, there's nothing to teach." He looked over his shoulder as his friends ran up behind them. "But you can follow." He took off running.

She wasn't as fast as him and the others managed to stay just ahead of her, but in no time her ability to heal put her in second place. It was a constant battle to repair the feeling of stinging bees in her overworked lungs as she raced through the city streets fighting to keep up with him.

They came to a six foot concrete barrier. Without hesitating, he ran halfway up, reached the top, and then vaulted over to the other side. She knew the others weren't far behind, so she charged at the barrier running as fast as she could. She tried to heave herself up but it was too smooth and she slid back down.

The others flew past her, vaulting the wall with ease. It was frustrating being the weakest. Healing the fatigue was easy but only practice was going to make her stronger.

She ran at the wall several more times certain that he was long gone. Finally, she pushed off hard enough to grab the top of the wall with one hand. Her fingers were slipping away just as her other hand came up and grabbed it. She pulled herself up and almost fell back down when she saw the entire group waiting on the other side.

"You've got to be kidding," Elaine complained staring directly at the dark haired boy. It was obvious he was the only reason they were still there.

Before Ada hit the ground they were off running again, over handrails, across picnic tables, weaving in and out of people and cars. Nothing got in their way. They used the city like an obstacle course.

As the sun disappeared behind buildings the others fell away until Ada was the only one following. He came to a stop in front of the building where they first spoke.

"You're a natural," he said.

"Thanks." She looked at her watch to hide her smile. "Wow, we ran for five hours."

"I'll be here tomorrow at noon." He turned to leave.

"Wait, you didn't tell me your name."

"Daniel." He stopped and stared at her again.

She bit her lip to keep from saying something stupid just to fill the awkward silence.

"Tomorrow," he said as he took off running and disappeared behind the building.

She turned and started walking home thinking about practicing and getting better and then remembered Madame Jardin and took off running.

11

It was dark by the time Ada reached the apartment. When she entered the living room, Madame Jardin was standing by the window with her purse in hand.

"Oh thank goodness!" She rushed forward embracing Ada. "I wasn't sure whether I should come looking for you."

"I'm sorry... I didn't mean to worry you." She was a bit dazed by Madame Jardin's concern.

"You're so dirty," she said lightly brushing off Ada's shirt and jeans.

"I was learning something important and I forgot about everything," she said, surprised at how filthy her clothes were as she followed Madame Jardin into the kitchen.

There was barely enough room for one person in the narrow kitchen so Ada pressed up tight against the counter as Madame Jardin bustled back and forth putting together a plate of food.

"Edith understands that you're a young girl with many things to do." She took the plate out to the table on the balcony.

"Edith?"

"Madame Cornot," she motioned for Ada to sit down and eat. "She waited for over an hour."

"Oh crap, I totally forgot." Ada looked at her watch. She hated disappointing Madame Jardin. "It's still early. Can I at least go down and say sorry?"

"It's late. It can wait until tomorrow." Madame Jardin sat down and motioned for Ada to come sit down.

"Please. I won't be able to sleep tonight," Ada said stubbornly standing in the doorway.

"Fine, fine. She will probably be in bed." She grabbed her purse and turned to face Ada, "But if she sees you like this she'll think you're going to make her sick instead of make her better."

Ada quickly cleaned herself up and then followed Madame Jardin down to the second floor.

Madame Jardin's stubborn knocking finally forced Madame Cornot to come to the door. After verifying they were who they said they were she opened and welcomed them into her home.

Ada recognized immediately the bitter odor of cancer, but was overwhelmed by a sharp chemical smell that hung in the air. The gaunt balding woman coupled with the suffocating smell brought back the sick feeling of the hospital visits and made Ada want to escape, so she sat down at the end of the couch closest to the door.

"The hospital's treatments can't tell the difference between the disease and me," Madame Cornot said apologetically organizing the few strands of hair left on her head.

"It feels like it takes me to the brink of death every time and what little of me is left fights to make a comeback, so I slowly shrink away to nothing." She stared quietly, fiddling with invisible threads on the couch. "The hospital people only see me as cancer, but I'm a woman, disappearing before their very eyes."

The nauseating smells were nothing compared to the agony Ada saw before her.

She stood, holding her palms upward toward Madame Cornot. "Can I put my hands..." but before she could finish her sentence Madame Cornot had already grabbed her by the forearms and held tightly, trembling.

"Make this leave my body," she whispered as she closed her eyes.

Ada knelt down in front of her. She could already feel Madame Cornot soaking in her energy. She relaxed and focused on healing the damaged cells coursing through the ravaged body. When a pungent sweat started streaming from Madame Cornot's pores Ada almost pulled away, but the determined woman's expression made her hold on.

Until this moment sickness and injury were just inconvenient annoyances that Ada had to observe in others on a daily basis, but now, in the hollow cheeks of Madame Cornot it wasn't just a disease trying to consume a body, there was a woman gathering what little she had left to make one last grasp at survival.

Instead of the normal release of energy that guided

the other person's system to heal itself, Ada radiated energy from her core that caused her hands and arms to slightly glow. Healing Madame Cornot felt different than the sluggish nerves and muscles of the boy at the sanatorium, or the confused and overreacting system of Janis from the church. Madame Cornot's immune system utilized the energy like an army receiving crucial intelligence that would win the war.

The ashen, sickly color of her skin faded. Slowly, Madame Cornot loosened her grip on Ada's arms until eventually she completely let go and lay back against the couch with her eyes closed. Her cheeks were fuller and the dark circles were gone. She was so still both Madame Jardin and Ada were afraid she might not open her eyes.

"You're a gift from God!" she burst out startling Ada and Madame Jardin. "Truly my dear, what you've done for me..."

Ada almost tripped backing toward the door, trying to get away from Madame Cornot who was now on her knees clinging to Ada's arm.

"No. Please don't do this..."

"Wait! Don't go." Madame Cornot stood and motioned them toward the kitchen. "I won't be able to sleep. Please have a cup of tea with me?"

After what turned into a full dinner with a famished Madame Cornot, Ada was finally alone in her room. She kicked off her shoes and lay back on the bed.

Running through the city streets for five hours

was far less tiring than the emotional drain that healing other people caused. She understood Madame Cornot's intense reaction but it was still exhausting just like the visits to the hospital with Jessie, and more than ever Ada didn't believe that duty played any part in who she should heal. She would heal who she wanted.

She flicked the light switch off and stared at the glowing circular face of the alarm clock. It was midnight. In twelve hours Daniel would be at the abandoned building.

She buried her face deep in the pillow, too bad she couldn't heal away the anxiety of having to wait.

12

Ada spent the first part of the morning with Madame Jardin touring Notre Dame Cathedral in a daze, thinking about what she would do differently when she ran with Daniel.

Cleaning the apartment while Madame Jardin was visiting Madame Cornot didn't make the time pass any faster, so she finished up and left early for the abandoned building.

It was an hour before Daniel was supposed to show up so she decided to check out the view from the rooftop. This time she ran up the wall and grabbed the second floor ledge a bit easier. Every time she pulled or pushed up her weight she healed her muscles, which was quickly making her stronger. Instead of turning around and jumping back out of the window she stepped down into a room the size of a small office. Grey pebbles and cement dust coated everything. As she brushed off her pants a startled pigeon flapped its way to safety in a flurry of wings and swirling dust.

It took a moment for her eyes to adjust to the darkness outside the office door. She opened doors to shed some light as she walked the hallway looking for a way up. Tucked back at the end of the hall she found stairs. With no windows and only the light coming from the door she left open behind her, the stairs were like climbing upward in a dark cave. She used the banister to guide her to the top until finally the darkness gave way to a thin blanket of gray light.

When she stepped out to the rooftop the bright sunshine made her squint and shield her eyes.

"You should be careful; some people call these buildings home."

She swung around to find Daniel behind her.

"I thought you'd be too sore to show today."

"I'm all right," she said sliding her hands in her back pockets. Usually she would look someone straight in the eyes to get an idea of their personality, but Daniel had these dark searching eyes that seemed to look straight into her mind. She walked to the edge and pretended to be interested in the building across from them.

"Where are you from?" he asked. Ada told him about Seattle and her last foster home.

"Are you running from your foster parents?"

She laughed at the thought of Dave or Carla looking for her.

"No, I just want to be able to get away from anyone if I need to, and you seem to be the master escape artist."

She stared out at the moving cityscape in silence. He hadn't taken his eyes off her. A few times she thought he might say something.

"What about you, why do you spend your days running away?" she asked turning to him.

"How do you know I'm not trying to be the best at chasing?" he smiled, "I've been doing Parkour non-stop for five years. It's what I love to do. About a year ago, when I was sixteen, I had a choice to go on with school and follow someone else's path or choose my own." He turned his back to the view and leaned against the wall. "So I work early mornings cleaning and stocking my uncle's store and during the day I run."

Voices from down below caught their attention. The guy and girl that were with him yesterday stood at the bottom of the building throwing stones toward the rooftop.

"And your friends chose the same?" she asked watching as the guy down below started running up the wall and flipping backward.

He laughed. "No. Florien and Elaine will go back to school when summer's over. What about you?"

"What about me?" she repeated contemplating.

She hadn't thought about school since the night Carla called Gretchen. There weren't any friends to miss; she never stayed long enough to make any. She liked staying with Madame Jardin, but once she found her mother, what then?

"I don't know. I really haven't thought about it." She answered a little anxious at the thought of leaving

Madame Jardin. He looked at her curiously but only nodded in reply. It didn't take long to appreciate the moments of silence Daniel liked to sink into.

"So, you ready to go?" he said standing. "Today, we work."

"And yesterday, that wasn't work?" she asked not sure if she could push herself any harder.

"If you want to be the best then we have to work on your landings." There was a six foot block shaped storage room in the center of the roof. He ran up the side and stood on the edge.

"I thought you said there's nothing to teach." She climbed up beside him smiling.

"There are a few things I can show you." He dropped off the side landing in a half crouched position and went into a roll. They spent hours working on landing. As Ada got better Daniel would move her to higher jumps.

By the end of the day Ada was jumping from the second story window and landing a perfect roll that she managed to come out of running. She no longer struggled hauling her own body weight. Her muscles were strong enough to allow some grace.

When they left the buildings and took to the streets Ada stayed tight on Daniel's heels. Only once she misjudged the height of a banister and caught her foot in midair, which sent her head first down a cement stairway. She was healed and halfway up the stairs when Daniel showed up at the top step.

The darker it got the more she tripped and fell. The knees of her pants were completely torn out. At nine she reluctantly told Daniel she had to go home. She knew Madame Jardin would worry if she was much later. They arrived at the abandoned building, alone. Florien and Elaine had long disappeared.

"I'll walk you home," he said starting in the direction of Madame Jardin's.

"It's kinda far," Ada said hoping that wouldn't change his mind.

"I know."

"How do you know?" she said speeding up to stay with him.

"Do you live with your grandma?" he asked with a sly grin.

She thought of the building across the way from Madame Jardin's balcony. It would be an easy climb for him. The windows had big ledges.

"You followed me?"

"I wanted to know more about you," he said.

"Not my grandma, just a really good friend." She looked down at the sidewalk so he wouldn't see her smiling, and then explained how she became friends with Madame Jardin.

The next few days were spent the same way, practicing climbing, jumping and landing. Ada felt like she was picking up fast everything Daniel showed her, until the fifth day. Instead of arriving before Florien and Elaine like usual, Daniel arrived with them. Ada figured they were bored with catering to her learning experience, and wanted to run without the lessons.

"Can you keep up?" Florien asked smiling.

"You might want to stay here and practice some more," Elaine said rolling her eyes.

Daniel instantly took off running. No place was sacred. They ran through busy streets, up and over walls, in and out of broken down buildings, dodging or using all obstacles at full speed. Ada realized they had been going easy on her. She lagged behind always bringing up the rear. She realized her muscles and endurance needed a lot more work. Sometimes she couldn't even see Daniel. Catching glimpses of Elaine's cropped yellow hair was her only way of keeping up.

After a couple hours of running she came upon Florien and Elaine sitting on a park bench. She looked around for Daniel. Florien nodded in the direction of a fifteen foot wide canal that had water rushing down it.

"He's on the other side. Elaine can't make it. I doubt you can either," he said leaning back.

Ada stood at the edge of the canal. The murky water left stains on the walls that contained it, and the summer heat gave it a swampy smell.

"You can go home now," Elaine said stepping onto the cement barrier beside her. Ada ignored her comment and eyed the wall from side to side trying to decide if she could make it.

"Give it up!" Elaine said laughing. "There's no way you'll make that jump, only the guys can." She stepped down nudging Ada with her shoulder. "Just, Go Home."

Ada wasn't sure if she could pull off jumping such a long stretch but floating down the river seemed a better exit than feeling Elaine's victorious glare on her back.

Ada brushed past Elaine as she gave herself some distance from the edge of the canal. When she stopped and turned around, Elaine's triumphant smile disappeared as she took her seat next to Florien.

"I can do this," Ada said aloud trying to reassure herself.

She ran as fast as she could toward the canal. The second her foot landed on the cement barrier, she pushed off strong. Halfway over, for a fleeting moment, she felt like she might make it, but when she slammed full force against the cement wall on the other side all she could think of was getting her breath back.

The unexpected jarring caused her whole body to tingle. Her nose and mouth were burning with the salty taste of blood. She managed to grab the top of the wall with one hand, healing herself as she dangled.

Her grip was quickly giving way as she readied herself for the water and the current.

Daniel's face appeared over the side as he tightly grabbed her wrist pulling her to the top of the wall.

"I knew you'd try," he said still holding onto her.

"So you're trying to kill me?"

"I thought you might make it."

"Might? And if I didn't?"

"I would've gone in after you." He gave her the grin again. "There are ladders up and down this canal. We just would've had to find one before the current smashed us against the grate at the end."

She shook her head at him. Florien and Elaine stood on the wall across from them.

"So that's how it's gonna be!" Florien yelled giving Daniel the finger as he turned and walked away with Elaine close behind.

"You made your friends mad," Ada said shoving her hands in her back pockets.

"They'll get over it." He wiped some blood from under her nose. The nose bleed and fat lip had already disappeared, but a little blood was left behind. She used her sleeve to wipe the rest.

Ada and Daniel ran through a new part of the city. Nothing was allowed to be a barrier. If she stumbled they went back to see how she could have done better.

By late afternoon Daniel had her convinced that all obstacles had potential for being tools that she could use to her advantage; she just had to reprogram her mind to see the tools instead of obstacles.

They came to an area with several twenty story buildings that all looked the same, rundown but not abandoned. The graffiti was angrier than the area around the building where they had first met. It was so thick the rough wall looked smooth with layer upon layer of spray paint. She couldn't always understand the words, but the occasional drawings gave clear definitions.

She followed Daniel to one of the buildings. It seemed, out of respect to the inhabitants, he ran the stairs to the rooftop instead of taking a more imaginative route. Ada was surprised to see a large crowd of people in groups talking, barbecuing and acting as if they were at a picnic in a park when in reality they were on the rooftop of a concrete building under a full moon.

Daniel grabbed her hand as they started through the crowd. She thought she'd be pushed to the side by all of the handshakes and half hugs, but he held her hand tight guiding her along. She noticed numerous girls looking her up and down, whispering and laughing. The pressing crowd started to feel like the tight walls of a dark cave.

Florien and Elaine showed up, motioning them to a corner, and for the first time Ada was glad to see her. Ada turned to face the city lights and relaxed enough to get a deep breath.

"He's pretty much ignored every girl here including me. That's why they're so interested in you, Daniel's *mystery girl,*" Elaine snorted.

Ada took a step sideways to get away from the sickening sweet smell of alcohol. She could sense the dull reaction of every cell and tissue in Elaine's body. Elaine slid down the waist high barrier to take a seat next to Ada's leg.

"Want some?" she asked slopping her drink in Ada's direction. Clear liquid soaked into Ada's pant leg.

"Nope," she said sitting next to Elaine.

Daniel and Florien were talking to a group of guys just down the wall.

"Yeah, I had a crush on Daniel and made a real fool of myself." She laughed and then was quiet long enough for Ada to hope she wouldn't have to hear the story.

"At one of these parties I cornered him in an apartment downstairs and took my shirt off. One too many of these." She held up the plastic cup rattling the ice back and forth. "He just shook his head and walked away. It took two weeks before I could face him again, and then he acted like nothing happened." She turned clumsily toward Ada. "Don't act like you haven't done something completely stupid when you were drunk."

"My stupid mistakes are done when I'm completely sober," Ada answered watching Florien do a back flip. The crowded space must be bugging him too, she thought.

"Florien's cute, but he acts like I'm just one of the guys," Elaine said, leaning her head against the wall and closing her eyes. "Please tell me the guy with the tattoo on his chest isn't coming toward us."

Ada looked up and saw a guy with no shirt and a large tattoo headed their direction.

"Baggy jean shorts and piercings?"

"That would be my ex, Vincent."

"He's coming."

Ada noticed Florien had stopped his acrobatics and was watching Vincent approach.

"Hey, let's go have some drinks downstairs." Vincent kicked Elaine's foot.

She finished off what was left in her glass and sighed, "sure, whatever."

"Wait. I uh..."Ada looked toward Florien again, but he'd already turned away.

"I'll be there in a minute." Elaine leaned back against the wall as Vincent headed toward the alcohol table.

"You're wrong about Florien. He's interested," Ada said, resting her hand on Elaine's shoulder to heal her polluted system.

Elaine sat up straight wiping the sweat from her forehead. The dazed look was gone. She turned to Ada with a puzzled expression.

"Come on," Vincent grumbled holding two filled plastic cups.

"No thanks, we're talking." She turned back to Ada.

"Don't screw around." He kicked her foot. "Come on."

"She doesn't want to go with you Vincent," Florien said walking toward them.

"Shut up Florien and get back to jumping around

like a fool." When they stood face to face Florien was around a foot shorter and 20 pounds leaner.

"Oh shit!" Elaine said jumping to her feet.

"Isn't it your brother that's crawling up community buildings and sneaking in people's apartments?"

"Don't say shit about my brother Florien." Vincent tossed the two cups behind him. "Maybe it's you guys who are sneaking around and then blaming Etienne for it."

Daniel came up beside Florien.

The argument was cut short when a group of five guys came over the wall in the front of the building. This seemed to ignite everyone on the rooftop.

"Speak of the devil," Elaine said shaking her head.

"Who's that and what's going on?" Ada said alarmed at the hostile reaction of the crowd.

"That's Etienne, Vincent's brother. He has his own Parkour group, but it's more like a gang. As you can see people don't want them climbing up the buildings they live in."

Florien and Vincent broke up only to join opposite sides of an even bigger argument.

"Stuff's been going missing," Elaine said as people crowded in front of them. "It's just stupid, and they think it has to be someone who does Parkour. We better get out of here. The cops'll be here any minute."

They slipped through to the middle of the uproar only to find Daniel and Etienne face to face. By the way Daniel's jaw muscle was flexed punches were about to be thrown.

Loud sirens sent people in every direction gathering food and bottles and then disappearing down the stairwell.

"Come on Daniel, we should go," Ada said urgently.

Etienne turned and looked her up and down with an unnerving smile. He was the same size as Daniel but the shaved head and tattoos made him look like a hardened criminal fresh out of jail.

Vincent pushed between them. "You gotta go man; the police are already here." He pulled Etienne toward a drain pipe running down the back of the building and they disappeared over the side.

Ada touched Daniel's arm lightly. The last thing she wanted was to become familiar with the French police. They waited in a hallway until they heard the police pass, and then snuck out the back of the building.

Few words were said while Ada and Daniel walked home. When they arrived in front of Madame Jardin's Daniel pulled Ada toward the shadowy wall of the building. They leaned silently against the cold stone until Daniel grabbed her hand.

"There's a place I want to show you," he said after a long moment staring at her.

"Okay," she said feeling the heat rush to her cheeks.

"After we run tomorrow," he said turning to leave.

Ada watched him disappear down a dark alley.

She felt like running after him, but Madame Jardin was waiting.

She looked up at the balcony light, warming the darkness. A thick drain pipe with metal rungs holding it in place ran up the side of the building. It didn't budge when she pushed against it. She could practice climbing and work through her fear of heights, she thought as she started upward.

Using the metal rungs and leaning slightly back from the pipe made it as easy as climbing a ladder. The rusty surface of the pipe helped with hand traction. At the fourth floor she could see the black iron bars of the balcony. She was pushing upward when one of the metal rungs creaked and gave way clanging to the ground below. She dropped a few inches before grabbing the pipe, hugging it tightly. It felt like the smallest flinch would cause her to lose her footing, so she hung there feeling her heart pound against the cold metal.

"Move or wait for the fire trucks to pry me off in the morning," she whispered aloud to herself.

The thought of telling Daniel she had to be removed from the drain of a building forced her to inch her way up while her other foot groped for the next rung. Her arms and legs trembled violently as she worked her way up the rest of the building.

Finally she felt the cold cement of the balcony and grabbed the bottom of the iron railing. She pulled herself up and fell into one of the chairs. Her heart pounded in her ears as she leaned back to catch her breath.

Raised voices coming from inside the apartment brought her back to her feet. Ada snuck toward the window to have a closer look.

"We just want to ask her a few questions," a man's voice boomed.

His back was facing her, so she couldn't see his face. She peeked through the window trying to locate Madame Jardin. She caught glimpses of her as the man paced, throwing his arms angrily in the air. The terrified look on Madame Jardin's face turned Ada's fear into anger.

"One way or another you're going to tell us," a woman's voice snapped.

Ada ducked to the side of the window when she saw Terry, the amazon woman from the hospital in Canada, walk up behind the couch.

She held a vial above Madame Jardin's head and nodded toward the man. "Pry her mouth open and I'll force the whole thing down her throat."

The man chuckled.

"We don't want to hurt you, but you will tell us where she is," Terry said resting her hand firmly on Madame Jardin's shoulder.

Ada pulled back from the window. Her heart was pounding so hard it made it difficult to breathe. She desperately scanned the balcony for a weapon. The amazon's heavy hand on Madame Jardin's frail shoulder made her tremble with rage. She spotted the cast iron pan Madame

Jardin used to fry eggs and grabbed it off the patio table. They can't hurt me unless I let them, she reassured herself as she clenched the pan's handle.

Hearing Madame Jardin's pleading voice sent her into the room. She lunged at the man as he turned toward her startled. The pan came down on the side of his head with a gong that made Ada's arm quiver up to her shoulder. She watched his eyes roll back as he fell to the floor.

Before Ada could turn to check on Madame Jardin, Terry leapt over the couch and grabbed her by the hair, but the pan was already in motion slamming down on the amazon's elbow. She screamed but still managed to sweep Ada into a head lock. Little raspy wheezes were all Ada could squeeze out from under her steel bicep. She scrambled to keep up as Terry swung around to check the unconscious man on the floor.

"Get up," Terry said, nudging him with her foot.

Ada could see by the injury that he wouldn't be waking up for quite a while. Madame Jardin's voice momentarily interrupted the struggle. She was frantically calling the police.

"Hang up that phone or I'll snap her neck," Terry hissed from across the room, grabbing a book from the shelf and throwing it at Madame Jardin. Her arm loosened slightly and Ada took full advantage twisting around and sinking her teeth into the muscular forearm.

"You little bitch, you bit me!" she screamed hurling Ada to the ground.

Terry briefly inspected her bleeding arm and then focused her attention on Ada. The wild look in her eyes made Ada scramble to her feet.

Ada lunged for the frying pan, but instead caught the full force of Terry's fist on her lower jaw. Everything changed to a blur in slow motion as she slammed against the ground. Muffled sounds were fading into a faraway silence when she realized she would be out cold if she didn't focus her mind on healing her brain.

Within a split second the heat was rushing to her head bringing her eyes back in focus. The scream of sirens echoed from the streets below. Terry was reaching to grab her by the hair when Ada landed an unexpected kick to her stomach. She fell to her knees gasping for breath. Ada lunged for the cast iron pan as Terry struggled to her feet and headed for the door.

A crowd of voices intermingled with Madame Jardin's echoed in the stairwell. Ada watched Terry hurry down the hallway and disappear into the other stairwell uncertain of whether to follow. Within a few seconds the hallway filled with police and concerned neighbors. Madame Jardin frantically rushed up to Ada.

The police searched throughout the building, but no sign of Terry. The unconscious man was being hauled away handcuffed to a gurney while Ada and Madame Jardin answered questions in the lobby.

It took another two hours for police to finish investigating before they were finally left alone. Madame Jardin closed the door and leaned against it taking a deep breath.

"I'm so sorry I got you messed up in this," Ada said standing in the dim hallway.

"No, no my dear, this is not your fault." Madame Jardin guided her to the couch. "You can't blame yourself for the bad nature of someone else."

"Remember how I told you about Jessie and the hospital in Canada? That woman was there...how did they find me?" Ada hugged her knees resting her forehead against them. "You're not safe here. You have to stay somewhere else for awhile. I can get you a plane ticket back to your daughter's." Ada swallowed the lump in her throat and tried not to blink to hold back the tears, but they slipped down her cheeks anyway. She hated crying.

"I have a sister in the south. She's always asking when I'm coming to visit. We can go visit her," she said, patting Ada's leg with a reassuring smile.

Ada shook her head no. "I won't mess your sister up too."

"What do these people want?"

"A slave who can keep them healthy," Ada said wiping her face and sitting up straight.

"You can't be alone," Madame Jardin said firmly.

"I have a friend. He'll help me." Ada told her about Daniel and what he was teaching her.

They spent the rest of the evening packing and talking. Ada promised to keep in touch through email.

Madame Jardin reluctantly caught a morning train to her sister's. She insisted Ada keep her key just in case, but Ada knew she couldn't go back to the apartment; someone would be lurking, at least for a while. Besides, it was time to do what she came to France for in the first place. She needed to find her mother.

13

Ada found a hotel close to where she was meeting Daniel. It was rundown on the outside but clean on the inside. The young woman behind the desk in the lobby hardly looked at her. It was early and Ada had interrupted a phone call. A quick swipe of her credit card got her a key to a room on the second floor not far from the stairs. An easy escape if she needed one.

A window at the end of the hall overlooked an alley. She leaned out to see if it was a dead end. Was this the pattern of the rest of her life, assessing escape routes?

She opened the door to a dark and stuffy room. It smelled like it hadn't been aired out in weeks. She started to unlock the window but noticed a cleaning crew scouring the street below, and dropped back behind the curtain to watch. When she started suspecting them of being spies for the senator she decided it was time to sleep. Exhaustion was messing with her mind. She grabbed a chair and braced the door. For now, this was how she had to do things.

Ada pulled out the pictures of her mother that the professor had given her, and lay back staring at the photos. The intensity in her mother's distant gaze made

Ada wonder, was it worry behind those eyes or just deep thought? She pulled her backpack close, using it as a pillow and fell asleep thinking about telling Daniel everything that had happened.

Ada woke to the sound of people in the hallway. She listened by the door while putting her shoes on. The voices disappeared, but the room already felt like a prison, so she grabbed her backpack and headed downstairs to check out.

On the street she struggled under the weight of her pack. There was no way she could run with such a load. She would have to find a place to put it. She still had over three hours until she was supposed to meet Daniel, so she tucked her passport in her back pocket and her bank card and money inside the leather booklet in the other pocket. There was a train station on the way to the abandoned building. It would have a storage locker.

The train station was packed with people. Ada found the storage area and picked a locker that she could easily see from the front doors. She stepped out to the sidewalk while stuffing the locker key deep in her pocket. There was enough time to take another look at the apartment building her mom was supposed to be living in. She decided to use what Daniel had taught her and run there as fast as she could without letting anything get in her way.

In no time Ada was standing across the street from the penthouse. A car couldn't have made it as fast as she did, she thought to herself. On the way she had one slip up using the side of a fountain to avoid a crowded sidewalk, her foot was still soaked.

After getting a glimpse of the doorman seated at his desk she walked the perimeter of the building trying to find another way in. There was a drain pipe but it didn't come close to a balcony or window. She didn't want to climb all the way to the rooftop with no certainty of an unlocked door.

She stood on the sidewalk watching the same crimson curtain ripple elegantly out of the open penthouse window. All of the windows leading up to the penthouse had a ledge of at least half a foot sticking out. Daniel made climbing them look easy but Ada knew, even with healing her tired muscles, it would be a difficult and scary climb.

She walked around to the back of the building and sat down on a step in front of the emergency exit. The building no longer looked elegant, but more like an impenetrable fortress. She rested her chin on her knees and tried to come up with a plan to get in. Breaking a first floor window was all she could think of.

The metal emergency door behind her burst open as two women with boxes of cleaning tools squeezed down the steps past her. Out of the corner of her eye Ada noticed the door about to slam shut.

Without thinking she leaned back and shoved her hand into the opening to stop the door from closing. She gasped at the few seconds of excruciating pain as the door slammed against her hand crushing her bones and slicing her skin, but the warm sensation of healing quickly overtook the injury. She was up and through the door before the ladies reached their car.

Stairs were directly in front of her. The murmur of voices drifted down the hall, so she waited until it was quiet and then shot across hoping the door to the stairs wasn't locked. It was open. She gently closed the door behind her and started up the flights of stairs. Her steps echoed, so she tiptoed and held the wooden handrail, but it rattled and creaked louder than her footsteps.

The doors were locked at the penthouse level, so she ended up in front of the same window as before looking up at the crimson curtain, but this time she knew she could climb up to the window.

Without looking down she stepped onto the ledge, turning so she was facing the window. All of the climbing and vaulting with Daniel had made her stronger. She took a deep breath and jumped just enough to catch the upper window's ledge with one hand, and then pulled herself inside the apartment.

Ada stood quietly checking out the room. A table trimmed with deep carvings and thick legs shaped like claws gripping the floor stretched over half the length of the room with several high back chairs tucked in around it. On top of the table were settings of lacy, white china. It looked like Dracula and the tooth fairy had come together to decorate.

There were two closed doors, one on the opposite side of the room, and the other to her right. She tiptoed over to the door across the room and put her ear against it to listen for voices or sounds, nothing except for the whisper of wind blowing the curtain behind her. Her heart pounded at the thought of coming face to face with her mother.

As she turned the knob it made a few clicking sounds that echoed through the silent apartment. She peeked in at a living room that stretched the length of the front of the building. A wall of windows overlooked the street below. It seemed like a showroom that no one really lived in.

She glanced around for anything that might offer a clue, a photograph, a piece of paper with her mother's name on it, but there was only a glass cabinet filled with untouched bottles of liquor, every other surface was meticulously clean.

A long hallway led to other doors. She carefully opened each and looked in. All were empty except a king sized bedroom at the end of the hall. Ada opened the closet and dresser drawers, no clothes or shoes. She sat down on the side of the bed, at a loss. The apartment was the only connection she had, and it was wiped clean; a front keeping her from finding her mother.

She opened a night table drawer. There were envelopes and a writing pad with the initials JM written in calligraphy. Jean Mechan, she mumbled to herself.

On the other night table was a phone. She was surprised to find a dial tone, but no number. She lifted the telephone to see if the number was on the bottom and found an address book hidden underneath. She leafed through finding a few names scattered throughout the book. At least it was something. She tucked it in the waist area of her pants and then decided to go back through the rest of the apartment to see if she had overlooked anything else.

Passing through the living room she noticed a small white device stuck to the side of a cabinet. On top of it was a flashing red light. Another one was on the wall tucked between the couch and an end table. Security devices. She rushed through the kitchen and back into the dining room where she counted two more. All she could picture was the police busting through the front door as she was trying to get out of the window. A faint click of a turning lock sounded in the other room.

She was straddling the window sill when a man poked his head in through the dining room door.

"No you don't!" he yelled, flinging the door open when he saw Ada halfway out the window.

She pulled her other leg over the sill and dropped down groping with her feet for the window below. She looked down to see how far off she was. When she looked up another man was in the doorway.

She recognized him from the pictures the professor had given her. It was Jean Mechan, the last man seen with her mother.

He stared back at her with an annoyed curiosity, while the oversized thug made his way to the window.

One foot had just found the sill as the man reached out to grab her. All she could do was aim and drop into the window below, but her foot slipped. She fell backward seeing the large head of the man poke out the window, watching her as she fell.

A breathless panic constricted her chest and throat. Scenery whizzed by like the landscape through a window in a bullet train. There was no healing herself if she was unconscious or worse, dead.

The healing heat burned through her entire body but nothing could have prepared her for the impact. She struck the ground with such force it felt as though her soul had snapped out of her body like a rubber band stretched to its capacity. She had to use all her energy to keep the darkness from closing in on the blur of watery images her eyes were trying to hold onto. She couldn't squeeze a breath out of her paralyzed lungs. There was crippling pain ripping through every nerve in her body. She struggled to keep her mind from straying into a sleepy dream.

A woman's face appeared in front of her. She could see her mouth moving but heard no words. There were so many places to heal her mind was muddled trying to reach them all.

The warm sensation of healing fought to reawaken a system bent on shutting down, but a black hole had already started closing in on the woman's face above.

With all that was left Ada reached forward grabbing the woman's shoulders. The moving mouth was the last image to disappear into darkness.

Only seconds had passed but it seemed like an eternity before air finally burst into her lungs. The face of the woman came clear as her voice screamed into Ada's ears. She lay there until everything was clear. The woman's words still sounded like she was talking with a mouth full of bubble gum, but when Ada heard what she was saying she realized everything was fine and rolled to her side and stood.

The woman kept touching her ears, "I was three when I ate an entire bottle of baby aspirin. I haven't heard a sound since. What's happening to me?"

Ada looked up and saw that the man in the penthouse window was gone.

"How can you be standing after falling like that?" the woman asked touching Ada's shoulder as if she might disappear.

"If they ask where I went, please don't tell," Ada said nodding toward the building.

"I won't," the woman answered picking the address book from the ground and handing it back to Ada. She felt her pockets to see if she'd dropped anything else.

Ada took off running and kept looking over her shoulder to make sure no one was following her long after the penthouse was out of view. She arrived in front of the abandoned building healing her exhausted lungs.

There was still time before Daniel was supposed to show, so she went to the roof.

She circled the top of the building double checking the ground below for any cars or people, and then sat down in a corner against the cool concrete and opened the address book. She kept thinking about Jean Mechan's cold glare when she was hanging out of the window. How could her mother have picked a guy like that?

She turned each page, but most of them were empty. Her stomach lurched when she saw three different telephone numbers and an address for Senator Grimes. A few pages after him, she found Professor Strathern's name and number. There were a few more names she didn't recognize, and then, on the very back page, a number for a Doctor Fautine at Trajet Lab. Altogether she counted nine entries. She wrote all of the names and numbers on the back page under the lab except for the professor and Senator Grimes. One of these people had to know something about her mother. She would start calling tomorrow after she figured out what to ask.

"Have you been here long?" Daniel asked.

Ada jumped to her feet and slipped the book into her back pocket.

"What happened to you?" He pointed to her shirt.

She was surprised to find the front of her shirt splattered with blood.

"There's blood on your face too, did you fall?"

He gently checked the side of Ada's head. There was a large patch of blood but no cut.

She shrugged and tried to wipe it off. He gave her a suspicious look. She wanted to tell him everything, even show him that she could heal, but she wasn't sure how to start or how he would take it.

Daniel gently grabbed her hand, "are you okay?"

Seeing the concern in his eyes reassured her.

"I..."

A loud crash sounded behind them. Florien and Elaine were standing in the stairwell doorway.

"This is what we're doing today, holding hands and staring at each other?" Florien grabbed Elaine and pulled her to him trying to kiss her neck. Elaine giggled and made a feeble attempt at pulling away.

"What were you going to say?" Daniel whispered in Ada's ear.

"I was just going to tell you that... I've been practicing a lot." She could see he wasn't convinced but loss of privacy made him leave it alone.

"You ready?" he yelled over to Florien and Elaine.

"I'm always ready," Florien answered.

Ada was surprised when Elaine came right up to her like an old friend, instead of the normal snide looks and rude comments.

"Hey," Elaine said, smiling.

"We'll stay above the city today," Daniel announced.

"Yeah, right on!" Florien said jumping up on a railing the size of a thin metal pipe.

Ada gave Daniel a puzzled look.

"The rooftops," he pointed out toward the buildings. "It's the quietest place to move."

And the most dangerous Ada thought to herself. Remembering the fall she'd just took made her stomach churn.

"We should show her the footage of the idiot who fell from the top of this very building," Florien laughed. "He thought he could make a jump this wide." He pointed to the next building over, which must have been thirty or forty feet away.

"You have to be a good judge of distance," Daniel added.

"Did the guy die?" Ada asked.

Florien laughed ignoring the question.

"He actually landed on his back but it didn't kill him," Elaine answered. "He broke a bunch of bones though. Let's just say he doesn't do Parkour anymore. He was in Etienne's gang. They shouldn't have been over here anyway."

"Do you like running roofs?" Ada asked Elaine as they followed Daniel and Florien down the stairs to find a different building to start at.

"Sure, if I don't feel good about a jump I don't do it. You can't do shit like you did the other day at the canal trying to follow Daniel."

Elaine ran ahead to Florien as Daniel hung back with Ada.

"You scared?" Daniel asked with an amused grin. She could feel him looking at her closely trying to catch some emotion.

"No, I just want to keep up."

It was time to conquer her fear of heights and one of the main reasons she wanted to learn Parkour in the first place, she reassured herself.

Ada stayed close behind Daniel. They ended up in an older neighborhood. The buildings were of similar height and separated by narrow streets or alleyways. Daniel picked a quiet alley and climbed up the back of the building using a drain pipe, Florien followed. Ada still didn't trust herself with heights, so she ran up the wall and grabbed the bottom of a fire escape. She was surprised to see Elaine following her.

"Don't hesitate, either jump, or don't," Daniel said to Ada after they all arrived at the top.

The first building they jumped to was a little shorter than the one they were jumping from and seemed only a few feet away, so Ada sailed with ease and landed smoothly.

She was so worried about jumping between buildings that she wasn't prepared for the obstacle course of garbage on many of the rooftops. A tangled clothesline sent her sliding on her hands and knees into broken glass but the cuts healed as quickly as she thought about them. She brushed the little bloodstained pieces of glass from her knees and hands.

When she looked up to see how far ahead Daniel was, he was watching her from across the roof.

"You okay?"

"Yep," she said running up to him. "Just tripped."

As the day progressed Daniel started practicing harder jumps. Distances between buildings were wider and drops to shorter buildings were steeper. She glided across an alley and saw her shadow pass over an old woman below looking up in amazement. They were forced to climb down some buildings because distances were too wide.

"I'm done," Elaine said as she started to climb to the ground. The sun was low in the sky, and they'd been going for several hours.

"You going to Leon's party?" Florien asked Daniel.

"No," he said glancing at Ada.

"Got it," Florien smiled as he draped his arm around Elaine's shoulders. "We'll be there, unless you got a better place."

"Nope, nothing," Daniel answered. "Meet at the store tomorrow morning."

"Yep," Florien said over his shoulder as he and Elaine disappeared around a corner.

"Are you hungry?" Daniel said turning to Ada.

She hadn't eaten all day. Healing didn't satisfy her hunger; it only smoothed away the nagging pain and any destruction caused by not eating.

"Yeah, I'm starved."

"Come on."

They walked and talked until they came to a small grocery. Daniel went right in, grabbed a basket and started filling it. Ada waited near the front looking at chocolate balls that had a toy hidden inside. She sat it down when Daniel came up. He grabbed two and tossed them in the basket. She was surprised to see bread, cheese, fruit and a type of meat she wasn't sure about in his basket. He sat it down on the counter in front of a man that seemed to be holding back a smile. He had tattoos of a torch on one forearm and a red haired woman in a bikini on the other.

"I'm glad to meet you Ada," the man said looking past Daniel as he put the groceries in a brown bag. "I'm Henri, Daniel's uncle." He had the same broad shoulders as Daniel, but he was thicker with graying hair and tired eyes.

Ada smiled and nodded, "nice to meet you."

"Hold on. You need something to drink."

Uncle Henri stepped out from behind the counter and disappeared down an aisle. He came back with two plastic wine glasses and a bottle of mineral water and slipped them carefully into the bag.

"Enjoy your evening." He handed Daniel the bag and refused to take any money.

"You work hard. I couldn't do it without you." He followed them outside to say goodbye.

Daniel led her to a park several blocks away.

They sat in front of a large fountain encircled by cherubs spitting water from their mouths. Street lights had just flickered on casting a warm hue, like candle-light through the park. The passing cars were the only reminder they were still in the city.

"Have you always lived with your uncle?" Ada asked.

"My Dad's from Italy. Three years ago he decided to move back and my mom went with him." He tore off a small piece of bread, laid cheese and meat on it and then handed it to Ada. "I've been living with my uncle ever since. Do you miss your home?"

"I liked Seattle. I really didn't have a definite home, only people I stayed with, well except for Jessie. She was different."

Ada went quiet thinking about Jessie. They had been keeping in touch through email, but the last few emails Ada had sent, Jessie hadn't written back. Was there a connection with what had just happened at Madame Jardin's?

"You alright?" Daniel asked.

She stared into his eyes. There was no doubt his concern was genuine, so how could she sit here and put him in such danger she thought, choking down the food. They would never stop coming after her.

"I shouldn't be here." She stood, looking around. "You're in danger if you're around me, just like Madame Jardin."

Daniel stood letting his food fall to the ground.

"What's wrong?" he asked grabbing her shoulders.

"For all I know they could be getting ready to storm the park right now." She looked at the passing cars and people.

"Who?" He looked around trying to see who she was talking about.

"I have to go. You should take a different way home." Ada backed up, but he grabbed her arm.

"Please don't do this. Just talk to me." He gently pulled her back toward the fountain's edge and sat down. "Please."

She sat down next to him. Being with Daniel was all she thought about, but even the smallest possibility of endangering him was unbearable.

"I can heal any injury, instantly," she blurted.

He stared at her silently for a few moments.

"That explains a lot. The falls, the blood, but not a scratch," he said smiling, but his expression turned serious. "Someone wants to hurt you because of this?"

"Yes."

She pointed to his left shin, "I can sense an injury, or whatever problem and heal it."

He looked down at the ground without saying a word and then rolled up his left pant leg revealing a large gash on his shin.

"I lost my grip on a pallet this morning. A nail was sticking out and it gouged my leg."

He turned to her curiously, "my uncle didn't even see me do it."

Ada kneeled down and laid her hand on the gash.

"I feel that," he said sounding surprised. His eyebrows rose when she lifted her hand and the injury was gone.

He pulled his leg up to have a closer look and ran his hand over where the injury would have been. The silence and his stunned expression made Ada nervous.

"Some people think I should be their personal slave. That's why I have to be the best at escaping," she said watching him. "And that's why anyone around me is in danger."

He took her hand and pulled her next to him. She told him what had happened the night before at Madame Jardin's and about her time with Jessie, and why she came to France in the first place.

Daniel stood and paced in front of her. She had no idea what he was thinking, but she was relieved to have told him everything.

He stopped abruptly, staring intently into her eyes, "you will be the best."

It was the first time anyone had made Ada feel safe; maybe it was possible to escape her stalkers after all.

"You shouldn't have to live in fear."

She smiled at his intense expression, "things were starting to look hopeless."

"You came here to find your mom, so let's find her."

"She's why I came, but not why I've stayed."

"Then stay with me. We have an extra room." He squeezed her hand. "You can't go back to Madame Jardin's, and they'll look for you at hotels." He leaned forward to see her lowered face. "My uncle won't mind."

"I can't do that to you guys. They were going to hurt her to get information about me." She clenched her teeth just thinking about it.

"No one will touch you at my place. We'd be gone before they got in the door. Besides, my uncle could show you a few things. He used to be a boxer."

She smiled, "I'm glad I met you."

Daniel gathered the food and put it in the bag, "you'll be ready the next time they come around."

After picking up Ada's backpack from the train station, Daniel showed her to his home which was an apartment above the store they had shopped at earlier.

He showed her into a simply furnished living room and then disappeared down a hallway. She went over to a window that pushed open to a view of the building across the street which looked identical to Daniel's except that it was a beauty shop. She felt a light pecking against her butt and whirled around to find a black German Shepherd that came up to her waist, sniffing her intently.

"Minuit is trying to introduce herself," Uncle Henri said from the doorway of the hall.

"So, Daniel tells me you're going to be our new roommate. Let me show you to your room."

Ada followed him to a room that Daniel quickly exited with an arm full of sheets. It had a single bed with a nightstand and dresser.

Minuit brushed past them, jumped on the bed and curled into a ball.

"I hope you don't mind dogs."

"I like dogs." She leaned her backpack against the nightstand and then took a seat next to Minuit. "Thank you for letting me stay."

"It's your room as long as you need it." He turned to leave but stopped. "Daniel said some people are giving you a bad time." Ada nodded. Uncle Henri had opened his home to her, so she felt it was only fair that he should know the danger.

"We'll teach you how to defend yourself."

Daniel poked his head in, "come on and I'll show you the rest of the place."

It was a small apartment compared to Madame Jardin's and way less cluttered. Daniel showed her the back stairway to the store and the roof. The rooftop was clean with a table and chairs and a few plants.

"I'm telling your uncle everything," she said.

Daniel smiled, "I'm glad you're here."

When they came back in the apartment Uncle Henri was reading a newspaper at the kitchen table. Ada pulled up a chair and sat down, careful not to kick Minuit who was asleep under it.

"The people following me are dangerous and they

wouldn't hesitate coming in your home and threatening you to find me." She explained what had happened at Madame Jardin's.

"Daniel mentioned it." He put the paper down and looked directly at Ada. "What do these people want with you?"

"It's better if I show you." She knelt down and called Minuit. Uncle Henri leaned over the table so he could see what she was doing.

Minuit's eyes had a milky film dimming the black area, turning it to a diluted grey. Ada placed both hands over Minuit's eyes and after a few seconds ran both hands down the dog's coat. Minuit gave one big shake from head to tail and then stood wagging energetically.

Uncle Henri came around the table knocking his chair backward. He kneeled in front of Minuit grabbing the dog's face in both hands.

"The cataract operation was too expensive." He pulled Minuit's face close to his, "her breath doesn't smell."

Ada turned to Uncle Henri, "I know your blood can barely squeeze through some of your veins and it's stressing your heart."

Daniel lifted the fallen chair and nodded for him to take a seat. Uncle Henri didn't take his eyes off Ada as he sat down in the chair.

"How do you know this and how did you..." he pointed to Minuit.

"I don't know, I just can." Ada held her hands out."I have to touch your chest. Okay?"

Uncle Henri looked so rigid sitting in the chair with his hands on his knees Ada and Daniel had to laugh.

"It won't hurt. I swear. I just have to touch you."

Ada pulled her hands away and Uncle Henri looked almost ten years younger.

"I feel it all over my body. This leg," he patted the left one, "It was numb all the time." He bent down and touched his toes. "My back," he stood up with a smile. "I've lived with pain for so long, I can't believe this." He turned with a serious expression to Ada who was petting Minuit.

"I figured if anyone came around to hurt you, an old fashioned beating would send them on their way. But this," he sat down on his chair. "This is different. Some might not want to give up."

"That's why I wanted you to know everything, and if you don't want me to stay, I completely understand."

"Ada, that room in there is yours as long as you want it." He turned toward Daniel, "and you were right, she's going to need to protect herself if she can't get away, and the sooner we start the better."

Uncle Henri pushed the few pieces of furniture in the living room against the wall and brought in some dusty, thinly padded boxing gloves and a padded mitt.

While waiting, Ada found internet access leaning out the living room window with her laptop.

She smiled opening an email from Madame Jardin. An animated silly looking cat popped up waving a paw saying "hello." To Ada's relief Madame Jardin planned on staying a month with her sister. Hopefully that would be long enough for the senator's thugs to realize she was long gone. She was disappointed that Jessie still hadn't emailed, but she figured she might be in a place like the cabins that didn't have internet access.

Uncle Henri came back in the room wearing some ancient sweat clothes and held out some gloves.

"We're going to focus on disabling your opponent instead of going toe to toe."

They sparred for three hours straight. He taught her kicks to the knees, chops to the throat, palm to the nose and knee to the groin or head. Every time Uncle Henri got tired Ada would heal him.

"I'll be in better shape than a twenty-year-old if we keep this up."

Uncle Henri tossed the gloves to Daniel and then stood behind Ada, "if you can hit him you can hit anyone. I've seen him wear guys out letting them swing and then when they're exhausted he delivers the damage."

Ada spent the next hour trying to punch Daniel, but never landed one. He would occasionally throw punches back at Ada that she usually dodged, but one landed on her jaw sending her into the waiting arms of Uncle Henri.

"Oh my God, I'm sorry," Daniel gasped rushing to her. She tried to convince him it was alright but he stopped throwing punches altogether and would only dodge hers.

After a late snack and talk at the table Ada said good night and went to her room. She lay in bed thinking and staring at the ceiling, too wound up to sleep.

Even though people were hunting her, she had never felt safer.

14

Ada waited until she heard someone moving around in the morning before she left her room. Luckily, they were early risers. The sun was barely up. Minuit had scratched at the door shortly after Ada had fallen asleep and then took up half the bed stretching out, but Ada enjoyed the company. Two hours was all the sleep she needed since she had become more efficient with her healing.

It was Sunday and the store was closed, but Daniel still cleaned and stocked, so Ada helped as much as he'd let her. When they went back upstairs Uncle Henri had breakfast laid out for them and almost as soon as they sat down they heard Florien yelling from the street. Daniel assured Uncle Henri that they'd be back in the evening with enough time to practice fighting.

As they stepped out the front door Florien made some strange whistling sounds while pointing at Ada and then back again to Daniel.

"She has her own room," Daniel said shaking his head.

"You mean your bedroom," Florien taunted as Daniel jumped the whole flight of steps trying to catch him.

"So you're staying here?" Elaine asked meeting Ada at the bottom step.

"Yeah, there was a problem at my other place, so Daniel said I could stay in their extra room."

"No need to explain," Elaine grinned suggestively as she took off running after Daniel and Florien who had both disappeared around the corner.

Ada rolled her eyes and followed.

They stopped in front of a tall building still in the process of being built, empty of workers. Some of the higher floors had walls but the rest were metal skeletons.

Ada leaned back to see the top, "you've got to be kidding. That's what, thirty stories high?"

Daniel and Florien were already on the second floor. There were no ceilings or floors only mazes of makeshift walkways.

Ada stepped inside the ground floor area looking for an easy way up. Small noises echoed like gongs throughout the place. Elaine rattled a heavy chain that locked a metal cage elevator causing Ada to whirl around to see what was going on.

"Too bad we can't ride this thing to the top," Elaine said slamming the padlock against the elevator door. Florien's voice echoed from above calling them to come up.

Daniel and Florien had used one of the smooth steel posts to run up and launch off. They then grabbed a beam on the second floor and pulled themselves up. Ada looked for an easier way and found a small forklift loaded with building materials that stretched up to a second floor beam. She caught the edge of the beam and pulled herself up. Daniel was standing in the center looking up through the open areas between the pathways. As Elaine came up behind her Ada watched Florien disappear up to the next floor.

"Please tell me we're not going to the top," Ada asked making her way to Daniel. "I don't like this place."

"We don't have..." before he could finish his sentence Florien came crashing down onto a steel beam, and then slipped through an open area slamming against the ground below.

"Oh my God, help him!" Elaine screamed as they all jumped down.

The way Florien hit the steel beam Ada knew he would be hurt, but when she got close enough and felt his energy fading she rushed forward and laid her hands on his head. She focused all her energy on his broken neck hoping the rest would heal quickly once it was fixed.

Elaine started crying when she saw blood gathering in a pool around his head, but what alarmed Ada was, despite her healing, his system was still trying to shut down. He wouldn't absorb anything from her and his energy was draining fast. She stopped trying to revitalize his system and started to concentrate on her own.

The burning came from the most inner point in her body and emanated to the surface of her skin like a force field.

Her hands against his head looked translucent like a touch of moonlight was trapped under her skin. His cells couldn't resist her energy. When she felt his system thriving again she turned her focus back to guiding it in the right direction. It was the longest she'd ever used her healing and the first time she had temporarily ignored the person's system.

Florien opened his eyes and lay there, staring straight up for a few moments.

"His eyes are open! Oh my God Florien, can you hear me?" Elaine fell to her knees beside him.

Ada stood up next to Daniel. He grabbed her hand and squeezed. An iron bar crashed to the ground behind causing them to whirl around. They heard voices echoing from above and saw Etienne step out from behind a beam on the third floor.

"That mother..." Daniel started toward Etienne, but Florien grabbed his leg.

"There's six of them up there. They jumped me from behind." Florien slowly stood and noticed the pool of blood on the ground and groped his head for a wound.

"Is that you Florien?" the voice echoed from above. "I knew you had a thick head, but standing after a fall like that it must be made of stone." There was a bunch of laughter.

"You're such an asshole, Etienne!" Elaine yelled up.

"Better shut your mouth Elaine or I'm going to let Vincent take what you dangled in front of him at the party."

"Let's just go," Ada said to Daniel who looked like he might start up there any second.

"They tried to kill him," he grumbled.

Florien stared at Ada for a moment as if trying to understand something.

"We can't fight his whole gang, and who knows what they'd do to them," Florien said nodding toward Ada and Elaine.

Ada stopped herself from saying that they wouldn't do a damn thing, because Daniel reluctantly started to leave.

They heard the incoherent yelling of Etienne's gang until they were well out of sight of the building. They stopped in front of the park that Ada and Daniel had eaten at the night before. It was early but everyone agreed to call it a day. Before they went their separate directions Florien stopped Ada.

"When I was out from the fall, I felt you in my head," he said staring intently at her. "I don't know what you did, but thanks."

She shrugged her shoulders and took off with Daniel.

Sparring for a few hours with Uncle Henri lightened Daniel's dark mood. Ada could tell by his intensity that all he was thinking about was catching up with Etienne.

When they were finished she showed Daniel the address book she had taken from the apartment.

She flipped to the back page where she had compiled a list of names. They decided to start with Trajet Lab. Maybe her mother worked there like in Portland with Professor Strathern.

They went to a phone far away from Daniel's. The memory of Mechan's cold stare and the senator's relentless stalking made her not want to take any unnecessary risks.

"You're trembling," Daniel said smiling at her hand holding the receiver to her ear.

"What will I say if she's there?"

A receptionist answered and asked how to direct the call. Ada stumbled, "uh, Simone Larue please." The line sounded as if it went dead.

"Hello?" Ada gave Daniel a puzzled look.

"Um... one moment please. Let me put you through to Doctor Fautine."

"I think she knows her," Ada whispered to Daniel. "She's putting me through." After a few moments of waiting Ada started to think she'd been disconnected.

"This is Dr. Fautine," an irritated voice grumbled on the other end.

"I'm looking for Simone Larue," Ada stated again with certainty.

"I'm sorry there is no one here by that name, goodbye."

"Wait, the receptionist said..." he hung up before Ada could finish.

After slamming down the receiver, she turned to Daniel, "we have to find Trajet Lab."

Ada and Daniel tried calling back the next day and asking the receptionist for directions but she either knew it was them or the location of the lab was a secret. The internet led them to some old news articles that accused Trajet Lab of horrific animal testing. All they had to go on was the name of the reporter, an Audrey Petite, but she no longer worked at the news agency that ran the story.

Ada took a seat on the curb while Daniel called different agencies they'd found on Ada's laptop hoping Audrey had only changed jobs not careers. After an hour of calling, he found her at a small feminist magazine. Ada scrambled to her feet and pressed her ear against the other side of the phone.

"Ms. Petite, I read your article on Trajet Lab and I was..."

"Who is this? If you read my article you must have read my retraction. I have nothing more to say."

"Wait Please!" the line went silent, so he started to hang up. "We'll call back," he said to Ada.

"That article destroyed my career," the voice on the other end of the phone answered.

Daniel almost dropped the receiver pulling it back to their ears.

"The cowards canned me because of it."

"I'm sorry, but my girlfriend came all the way from America looking for her mother and Trajet Lab is the first lead we've found."

"If she's involved with them, and you can't get a hold of her, God help her. What they did to those animals..." her voice broke off.

"We need an address. Do you..."

"I know it was the CEO, Jean Mechan, who threatened my parents. They're seventy-years-old for God's sake."

They heard drawers slamming and rustling papers.

"You'll be on your own, even the police will turn a blind eye."

"We won't mention..."

"Oh believe me, I will deny ever having spoke to you," she snapped. "10 Rue Mepris."

The buzz of dial tone ended the conversation.

"I'm starting to hope Trajet Lab isn't a lead after all," Ada said watching Daniel hang up the phone.

"We better go find out."

15

Trajet Lab was located on the outskirts of Paris. They took the metro most of the way, and then ran the rest. Neighborhoods changed to industrial parks packed with warehouses and trucks loading and unloading. When they came to the street the lab was on there was no traffic or people. It was like a street from a ghost town. Every building they passed was empty even the ones across the street and not an address to be seen.

"This can't be right," Ada said, but then quickly held her hand out to stop Daniel from going forward.

"Look," she pointed to a camera mounted on the corner of the building just ahead. It was slowly scanning its way back toward them.

Daniel pulled her into a door well, "good catch. Let's check it out from the roof." He pointed to the building across the street.

They went around to the back making sure to stay out of the camera's view. The fire escape was too high for her and she couldn't see anything that would help her reach it.

"Can't set your mind on one way." He ran up the

wall and then pushed off of a drain that she hadn't noticed and grabbed the bottom of the fire escape.

The lab was the shortest building on the block only four stories high. There were cameras on each corner including two on poles monitoring the roof.

"Looks like a jail," Daniel said. The few windows were one way only reflecting the world outside.

"This place creeps me out. I hope she doesn't work here," Ada said.

"We're going to have to go in to find out. But for now let's just watch."

An hour had passed when a security guard came out the front door and walked the perimeter of the building. He seemed bored and paid little attention to anything except his cigarette.

By the end of the night Ada and Daniel counted two guards that patrolled the building every hour and a half. They were about to leave when a group of four people came out the front door and walked to a parking lot on the other side of the building.

"Ten O'clock, shift's over," Daniel said. "Tomorrow Florien and Elaine can watch from there." He pointed to a building across the street, "and then we'll figure a way in."

Ada watched the guard crush out his cigarette before he went back inside, and wondered how Daniel could sound so certain.

The next morning, while Daniel was working in the store, Ada went and bought walkie-talkies and binoculars for everyone. If something went wrong they'd at least be able to communicate.

She was sparring with Uncle Henri when Florien and Elaine showed up. The more questions Florien asked about her mother and the lab the more Ada wished she hadn't involved them. Daniel met them out front with a backpack slung over one shoulder.

"We'll be there a while, so I grabbed some food."

They picked the two vacant buildings diagonally across from each other to start their watch. Florien spent the first few hours goofing around on the walkie-talkie. Ada and Daniel turned their volume down so no one would hear.

It was dark when they all met up at the building Daniel and Ada were in. Hours of staring at the lab, and seeing nothing except the security guards making their rounds, was getting boring.

"You really think you'll find something about your mom in that fortress?" Florien asked climbing through the window.

"I don't know," Ada said sliding down the wall to sit. "They recognized her name and then just blew me off pretending not to know her."

Florien shook his head, "this place is serious, surrounded by empty buildings, cameras, security guards."

"Did you see the cars those guys were driving?" Elaine added as she sat down next to Ada.

"No shit, you should see the killer BMW the old dude drives," Florien said as he turned to Daniel, "how long till we make our move?"

"We have to find a way in," Daniel said as he tossed him the backpack of food.

"They only use the front door and each person has a badge they swipe to open it," Elaine said resting her head against the wall with closed eyes.

"Keep watching. We'll meet back after the night shift leaves," Daniel said going back to the window.

Ada watched Florien and Elaine disappear down a dark alley below and then went back to Daniel at the window facing the lab.

"The roof seems like our only shot," she said.

"Maybe, let's just give it a little longer."

Ada and Daniel watched the last of the night shift disappear around the corner of the building toward the parking lot when Elaine's panicked voice came over the walkie-talkie.

"Florien's not back! He went to pee, but it's been too long. I tried to get him on the walkie-talkie, but he won't answer."

They checked the alleys and the bottom of the building before meeting up with Elaine at her building.

"Heard anything?" Daniel asked.

Elaine shook her head and tried the walkie-talkie again.

"What if they know we're here and snuck up on him?" Elaine nodded toward the lab.

"We'd have seen something," Daniel said stuffing Florien's things in his backpack. "He's around here. Maybe he just got tired."

"Who's tired?" Florien's voice came from the window behind them.

"You bastard, we thought something happened." Elaine threw a box of chips at him as he climbed in.

"I had to get this." He tossed a plastic card to Daniel. Ada peeked over Daniel's shoulder to see what he had. It looked like a credit card except it had a large clip on top and the words Trajet Lab across the front. A picture of a grey haired man with the name "Dr. Jaques Fautine" was written under it.

"It's one of their badges." Daniel looked at Florien in amazement. "How'd you get it?"

"I was checking out that black beamer. The idiot keeps a key in a magnetic box above his back tire. I was looking around the car when I heard voices. I thought for sure he'd see me when he got in the car, but he started driving home. Pulls into a parking garage about ten minutes away clips that..." he nodded toward the card, "to the dashboard and leaves. He might as well of just handed it to me."

"Right on man." Daniel handed Ada the badge. "We have to do it now. Before the old guy realizes his badge is missing."

The plan was simple enough: Florien and Elaine create a diversion so Ada and Daniel could sneak in, but Ada kept thinking of all the things that could go wrong. Once inside they would check offices until they found information, and then leave through whatever way was easiest. They mapped escape scenarios while waiting for the security guards to do their patrol.

"Guard's in, we need to move now," Florien said tossing a pop can to Elaine and then shaking two violently and shoving them in his pockets.

"A face full of that will piss them off." He nodded toward the can Elaine was gripping nervously. "Don't worry, they'll only chase us so far."

Ada and Daniel stored the backpacks on the rooftop, and then stood in the door well watching as Florien and Elaine crossed the street toward the front door of the lab. On his way Florien ran up the corner of the building and ripped out one of the cameras smashing it to the ground. Elaine hurled her can at the front door exploding pop all over the glass.

The first security guard burst out the front door as Florien popped the top of his can spraying it in the guard's face. His second can struck the forehead of the second guard as he poked his head out the door to see what was going on. Elaine kept her distance as Florien juked between the flailing fists of the guards, until they took off around the corner with both guards in hot pursuit.

Ada and Daniel ran for the door, key card in hand. They could still hear the distant shouts of the security guards.

"There's no way they'll catch them," Daniel said swiping the card through. The locks clicked and Ada pulled open the door. Cool air conditioning swept around them. They moved quickly past the security desk glancing to see if cameras were also monitoring the inside, but the screens only showed the outside of the building.

A long entry way branched off in two directions of hallways. They made their way down the darker one. The first door they opened was a janitor's closet filled with cleaning supplies and a sink. Daniel listened at the next door and then opened it slowly. It was an office. The sound of the emergency exit made them slip inside, and Ada quickly shut the door behind them. She barely took a breath afraid someone might hear her pounding heart. They listened to the thump of feet pass outside the door. She looked at Daniel and couldn't help but smile. It was amazing at a time like this he could be giving her that grin that made her want to melt.

"You enjoy this too much," she whispered as they started quietly opening drawers and looking through papers.

They found nothing relating to her mother, only a lot of paperwork documenting clinical studies.

"This must be what that reporter was talking about, look." She pointed to notes written at the bottom of a lab report.

Serum SL272 batch 97- Canine response to sustained injuries has no significant immune response, if anything slight delayed reaction.

All of the drawers and a filing cabinet were filled with dated folders packed with the same type of reports. She shrugged her shoulders and put everything back as it was.

Daniel opened the door a crack to make sure the hallway was clear and they quickly slipped into the next room. It was empty along with the other three rooms in the hallway.

"We have to cross to the other hall," Daniel said.

Crossing meant passing through the entryway hall that the security guards' desk sat at the end of. She stayed right up against Daniel as he looked around the corner at the guards' desk. He reached behind and took her hand. Before she had time to worry they were in the other hall. More empty rooms lined both sides. At the end of the hall was a door to a stairwell. They peeked in and saw stairs going up and down.

"Let's start at the bottom and work our way up," Ada whispered.

They were just about to step through when Ada felt a hand lock onto her shoulder. Before she realized what was happening she was flung against the wall behind her. One of the security guards with a scraggly ponytail shoved Daniel inside and slammed the stairwell door closed, bracing his foot in front of it.

He held Ada pinned against the wall by her shoulder. She heard Daniel slamming against the door trying to get it open.

"I got this one, but there's another one on the stairs," the guard yelled over his shoulder to a tall, thick oaf of a man coming down the hall toward them.

"Run Daniel!" was all Ada could get out before the security guard's hand forcefully covered her mouth, slamming her head back against the wall. She bit down as hard as she could.

"Son of a bitch!" he yelled yanking his bloody hand from her mouth.

"You need help with the little girl, Louis?" the tall guard said laughing as he walked past and opened the stairwell door. Ada heard something slam hard against the wall and then it was quiet.

"Your boyfriend is the least of your worries now," the guard said.

Ada stopped staring at the door and focused her attention on the guard who was keeping her from helping Daniel. As the guard reached up and grabbed a handful of her hair, Ada landed a knee to his groin. She was ready to land another one, like Uncle Henri had taught her, but a back hand to the side of the head sent her rolling across the ground. The metallic salty taste of blood filled her mouth. She jumped to her feet and tried to smash his nose with her palm, but he easily batted her arm away and threw her against the wall. Her brain rattled and chest tightened as she gasped for breath, but she instantly healed it away.

"You got heart," he said smiling, unbuttoning the top two buttons of his shirt. Ada took the opportunity and smashed her palm as hard as she could up into his nose. He stumbled backward as blood burst across his face and the palm of her hand.

"You're gonna regret that," he said grabbing his nose and looking at the blood covering his hand. "You want it rough..."

She cut him off with a punch to the neck and then snapped out a kick to his chest. He grabbed her by the hair and pulled her into his swinging fist. It landed above her right eye causing her knees to buckle and sending a wave of nausea through her. She felt the skin above her eyebrow split and saw a stream of blood spray in the air. With a self-satisfied smirk he stared at the open wound above her eye and then followed the blood to the ground. When he looked up Ada landed another punch to the nose followed by a knee to the groin. He backed up with his fists raised, staring in dismay at the area above her eye where the gash should have been.

"You're like that freak downstairs!" he said his eyes flashing.

Ada brought her fists up and stepped one foot slightly forward.

"Let's see if you're as fun," he growled.

One punch after another pounded her to the ground. She tried to cover her head as he hovered above continuing to pummel her until his face was a blur of anger. She could barely catch a breath, but continuously managed to repair her battered head.

Finally, he stepped back panting. The look in his eyes turned wild when she stood wiping the blood from her face onto her sleeve, fixing her broken nose right before his eyes. He let out a chilling war cry and then charged at her again. Her heart raced afraid that she might not be able to keep up with the barrage, but instead she only got faster at healing the damage. His exhausted gasps and grunts gave her hope. She realized it was only a matter of time and he would be out of energy. She sensed his fatigued body as he used his last bit of strength to pick her up and hurl her against the wall, so hard that the drywall sucked inward on impact.

He staggered backwards and leaned against a door gasping for breath. Ada jumped to her feet and rushed forward kicking him in the groin. When he buckled over in pain, she put all her weight behind a knee to the face that knocked him out.

She knew it would be a while before he came to, but just in case she used the handcuffs on his belt to secure him to an old radiator. It wouldn't be easy getting out of that she thought as she locked the cuffs. She pocketed a loaded key ring, and pulled a baton from a loop on his belt and then ran to the stairwell. An angry yell led her to the roof.

Opening the door to the rooftop she saw the second guard dragging Daniel's limp body toward the edge of the building. Daniel's walkie-talkie was on the ground in front of her. She grabbed it and threw it against the back of the guard's head. He turned with a surprised expression and let go of Daniel.

"You! Louis let a little girl get away from him? Your buddy was just about to take a fall."

He pulled a taser off of his belt. "Thought he had me and turned his back too soon."

Ada looked at Daniel then back to the guard and readied her baton. He let out an echoing laugh.

"I'm gonna spend time on you," he smirked as he fired the taser. The prongs latched onto her chest bringing her to her knees. Waves of pulsing pain battled against her healing. She moaned struggling to raise her violently trembling arm and ripped out the taser prongs.

"Must've broke on your boyfriend." He threw the taser at Daniel, and pulled the baton from his belt.

Ada took a breath and held her baton ready.

"You've got to be kidding," he said, laughing loudly. "Well, show me what you've got."

Ada charged before he could finish his annoying laugh. With all her strength and weight she slammed her baton against the side of his knee as his baton struck the middle of her back with violent force. He fell to the ground holding his knee. She stood and faced him ready for another assault.

"What the hell!" He held up his hand for her to stop, "that would've crippled a grown man." He stared at her, cradling his shattered knee. "You're like the woman in the basement." His voice lowered to a pleading. "I don't want trouble. I was just paying the bills. Jobs are hard to come by especially when you've done time."

"Strip down to your underwear and handcuff both your hands to that pipe." She pointed her baton toward a sturdy pipe secured like a handle into the cement wall beside the door. She moved toward Daniel and watched the guard painfully do everything she'd said.

After he had clasped the last handcuff Ada kneeled down and rested her hands on Daniel's head and chest. His face was swollen and bloody. She watched the damage fade and smooth under her touch.

Before his eyes completely opened he mumbled, "I'm sorry Ada," and turned to look at her.

She smiled and used her sleeve to wipe some of the blood away. He stood and then noticed the guard handcuffed to the pipe.

"I was just doing my job man," the guard pleaded.

Daniel turned and looked at Ada, impressed, "you're getting tougher."

"No, just more endurance," she smiled. "They both mentioned a freak like me in the basement."

"Let's go."

"Hey, why don't you fix my knee like you did his face?" the guard asked leaning against the wall to keep the weight off of his knee.

"How about I kick and punch you a few times while you're down like you did me," Daniel said as they started toward the basement.

The door to the basement was locked, but after trying several of the keys on the guard's key chain Ada managed to unlock the door. Another corridor led to another locked door. They could hear dogs barking from a room in the hallway ahead. When they opened the door the smell was staggering.

Ada walked in and was knocked backward by the eye watering stench of urine and feces. Daniel flipped on a light and stood beside her. The barking and cat cries were deafening until she moved further into the room then they turned to whining groans. There were rows of cages too small for the inhabitants. Most of the animals were severely injured and some were long dead adding to the overwhelming smell.

"This is so wrong," she said not sure where to start. "I hate these people. I won't leave until we help every one of these animals." Ada said reaching for a cage.

"Let's finish looking, so we can herd them all out at once," Daniel said taking her hand.

Ada reluctantly closed the door to the wailing animals. Her chest tightened at the thought of her mother in this place.

A thick metal door at the end of the hall was marked with a danger sign. They found the key and entered cautiously.

It was a lab filled with more machinery than Professor Strathern had at the university. Large jars filled with yellow fluid lined several shelves on one of the walls. Ada went over to have a closer look. Each jar had something floating in it. She read the label stuck to the middle of the first jar, *SL1-Regenerated Kidney.*

"Daniel come look at these," she said reading the next few labels. There were three jars marked regenerated kidneys. The next few jars were the same except they were holding spleens.

"Pickled body parts," he said from behind her.

"Regenerated ones," she said afraid to think about what it might mean.

Another wall held hundreds of small vials marked with the same serial numbers they saw upstairs on the lab reports. All were stamped with "serum failed."

"Check this out," Daniel said trying to open a glass door at the back of the room. Black plastic covered the glass so they couldn't see in. Ada tried every key but none fit.

"I hate this place," she said pressing her forehead against the glass of the locked door.

"Hold on." Daniel grabbed the baton that Ada had left on a counter when they came in the room. He motioned her to get back from the door and then smashed the window out, reached through and unlocked it.

"Come on," he said opening the door.

She followed him into the dimly lit room packed with more equipment. A platform in the center of the room held an operating table with lighting propped around it. As she came closer she realized someone was strapped to the table. She froze staring at the profile instantly recognizing it was her mother.

Simone was in a full body straight jacket that was bound and locked to the table. She couldn't even turn her head to see who was looking at her. Ada felt Daniel come up behind.

"It's her," she whispered stepping onto the platform. She could see her mother's eyes straining to the corners to see who was in the room.

"Oh my God," Ada gasped. Simone's lips were completely sewn together. By the excitement in her eyes Ada knew she recognized her.

Startled by her gasp, Daniel rushed up beside her, "let's get her out of this."

Her mother's eyes went from excited to suspicious when she saw Daniel.

Ada started trying to undo the straps, but each one was held tightly by a small padlock.

"The keys are probably around here," Daniel said opening drawers.

Ada turned to search, but her mother started shifting and making noises. She motioned with her eyes toward a wall on the other side of her. Hidden behind a lab coat was a long shoestring with several small keys dangling from it.

"They're here," Ada said over her shoulder to Daniel and then rushed back to her mother's side.

They unbuckled the straps binding her upper body. Simone took over the second her arms were free. She pulled the cap off revealing a shaved head. Ada continued undoing the straps on her feet.

Ada and Daniel stepped back when Simone jumped up, and pulled apart the stitches binding her mouth. The holes healed before the strings were barely out.

"Ada?" she said reaching for the lab coat to cover her short hospital gown. "Did they find you too?"

"Huh?" Ada said confused.

"You came here of your own accord?" Simone asked buttoning the coat. "How old are you now?"

"Uh, fifteen," Ada stammered.

"Aren't you crafty," Simone said over her shoulder as she went to a computer hidden in a desk and started typing and then writing things down.

"We should probably get moving," Daniel whispered close to Ada's ear.

Simone spun around on the computer chair and stared directly at Daniel with an unreadable expression.

"Aren't you a looker. I'm sure you're used to running the show, but at the moment I need to retrieve some information." She spun back around and continued to type and write.

Ada felt the heat fill her cheeks. Daniel looked surprised but played it off.

"We'll be down the hall," Ada said aloud, grabbing Daniel's hand and leading him to the hall toward the caged animals.

"Sorry, she shouldn't have said that."

"Doesn't matter," Daniel said opening the door while Ada flipped on the light.

"I have to heal them first." She went to each cage and touched the horrified animal inside healing the wounds. "They're starving."

"I can help with that." Daniel disappeared behind a row of cages and came back with a large bag of dog food and followed behind Ada pouring food in the cages.

Most animals welcomed her touch. Only a few bit down in fear, but quickly let go when the warm energy wiped away the pain.

After the last cage Ada stopped, "if we close the door and let them loose in here, we can herd them all out at once."

Daniel smiled, "sounds good."

In no time the room was full of roaming dogs and cats, too distracted by freedom to be aggressive. They propped open all of the doors leading to the front door and then went back to let loose the animals.

Simone was standing near the door with a disgusted look on her face.

"Are we done playing animal rescue?" she said as Ada opened the door and animals raced past.

They came to the corridor where Ada had fought

the first guard. The stampede of animals over the top of his body woke him up.

"Well done," Simone said turning to Ada. "Hello Louis," she bent down grabbing him by the hair so they were face to face.

"Oh Jesus," he said trying to pull his arm free from the radiator.

"I'm not tied down anymore, you filthy pig." Simone slammed his head against the ground. "Now let's see if those disgusting visits were worth it."

"We better go," Ada said startled by the look in Simone's eyes.

"Wait for me outside," she commanded. Her icy expression warned against arguing.

"I was gentle. I never hurt you," Louis pleaded as they walked away.

The fresh air from the open front door drew the animals out sending them in every direction.

"At least they won't be tortured," Ada said as the last few stragglers made their way out the door. They heard the pounding of tennis shoes on pavement as Florien and Elaine came sliding around the corner.

"We've been trying to find a way in this dungeon," Florien said catching his breath. He handed Ada and Daniel their backpacks.

"I was at the top of that building," he pointed to the building across the street, "when that guy tazed you in the back. I thought about trying to jump it, but I'd be no help dead. Then I saw her show up." He laughed pointing at Ada, "like a super hero!" He started to describe the event when Simone showed up in the front doorway.

"We need to go," she said sizing up Elaine and Florien with her icy stare. "Alone. The troubled teen days are over." She turned to Ada, "come on."

"These are my friends," Ada said defiantly.

Simone raised an amused eyebrow. The lab coat and hospital gown were replaced by jeans and a brown leather jacket, both too big. A tan carrier bag bulging with papers was slung over her shoulder. She turned and started walking down the street.

"So, that's your mom?" Florien asked.

"Hey, we'll meet at the store," Daniel said nodding at Florien.

"Thanks you guys," Ada said. She felt like she should be leaving with them.

"Take care of yourself Ada," Elaine said as she took off after Florien.

"You better go," Daniel said looking in Simone's direction. "She's probably pretty messed up after all she's been through."

Simone didn't seem like the type someone would feel sorry for, Ada thought glancing at the fading silhouette of her mother.

"I get the feeling if I don't go after her I'll never see her again. I'm not sure why I care, but you know."

Daniel nodded.

"Call me when you can," he said touching her hand gently. "Be careful."

He took off running. A heavy knot of anxiety settled in her stomach as she watched him disappear wanting to follow, but instead she turned and ran in Simone's direction.

"I suppose it's reunion time for us," Simone said as Ada approached from behind.

"Was it Jean Mechan who trapped you like that?" Ada asked ignoring the condescending tone. Simone picked up the pace so Ada had to occasionally jog to keep up.

"I guess it's none of my business," Ada mumbled.

"Better be careful, the handsome ones can't be trusted," she said coming to a stop and turning to Ada. "Actually none of them can be trusted. As for Jean, every action has its consequence, and be assured I will take back from him what he took from me."

The flash of anger in Simone's expression made Ada step back then she remembered all of the pickled organs in the jars at the lab and gasped. Simone started walking briskly again.

Ada quickly caught up, "he thought dissecting your organs would give him the secret to healing?"

"Monsieur Mechan is far greedier than that. He took them for himself. They're in his body and I will have them back."

"And you were able to regenerate new ones." Ada

fell behind considering the possibility, "that's amazing."

Simone stopped abruptly and faced her with that prying gaze, "I'm glad you're impressed." She gently tucked a strand of hair clinging to Ada's cheek behind her ear. "Do you have money? I can't access my accounts until the bank opens in the morning."

"Yeah, I have some," Ada answered shaking her hair free. "Did his experiment work?"

"Be assured, I wouldn't be standing here if it did."

They walked for over a half an hour until Simone stopped in front of a small but elegant stone building. Ada couldn't stop thinking about Jean Mechan and the lab. What would they do now that nothing was left to torture?

"This is acceptable," Simone said walking up the steps to the hotel.

Instead of a room they rented a small but richly decorated apartment. Simone took the bedroom with its own private bathroom while Ada took the couch in the living room that was also a pull out bed. Simone disappeared for over an hour before coming out in a towel and seating herself at a desk near the couch. Ada could still smell the faint stench of the caged animals on her clothes and thought about how nice a hot shower and washing machine would be.

"I'm not one for small talk," Simone broke the silence. "What is it you want from me?"

Ada felt her cheeks grow hot. "Nothing," she stumbled. "They said you disappeared, so I decided to find you." She started unfolding the couch into a bed.

Simone sat silently with an amused grin watching her.

"Mission accomplished," she smirked. "When you say *they*, you mean Jessie I'm sure, and who else may I ask?" The menacing smile and demanding tone made Ada not want to mention Professor Strathern.

"So why'd you dump me off with Jessie in the first place?" Ada said, setting down on the edge of the bed so she was face to face with her mother.

"You won't be happy with the answer, but I'm a firm believer in brutal honesty, so here it is. I didn't want kids and I didn't intend to get pregnant, but accidents happen and believe me I tried to handle it myself treating it like an ailment and trying to heal it away."

"You mean me, not it," interrupted Ada curtly.

Simone continued, "I even sought medical help, but obviously you were as willful in the womb as you are now." She went to the window moving the curtain slightly to see the street.

"I met Jessie through a mutual benefactor. I knew a few days of diapers and bottles, and she'd be hooked." Simone pulled up a chair next to the couch.

Ada remembered the conversation with Jessie at Professor Strathern's, and now understood what Jessie meant by being too busy to look for Simone.

"Why not my father?" Ada grumbled sitting back against the rollaway, so she didn't have to see Simone's smug look.

"Father," she laughed. "Think of it this way, now you have someone to blame for all of your problems." She returned to the window. "I'm sure you were looking for a mother's shoulder to cry on, but you're better off taking care of yourself. My philosophy is..."

"Save it," Ada interrupted jumping to her feet. "I see the source." She had to fight back the lump in her throat as she slipped on her shoes. A raised eyebrow and forced smile betrayed Simone's composure. Ada grabbed her backpack and stopped just before the door.

"Good luck with that Mechan guy, sounds like you guys have a lot in common, you're both really good at torturing." Ada slammed the door behind her.

She didn't realize how stuffy that room was until she stepped out into the cool night air in front of the hotel. She ran fast and hard to Daniel's, without looking back. The streets were empty except for a couple of homeless people huddled on the sidewalk sleeping. Anxiety didn't heal away, but running made her feel free and strong.

By the time she arrived at Daniel's, she was ready to file Simone away with the rest of her bad memories. She didn't want to wake Uncle Henri, so she climbed the outside wall to Daniel's room. The lights were still on.

He was lying on his bed listening to music. She tapped on the glass lightly. Seeing him rush to the window made her heart heavy.

"What happened?" he asked helping her inside.

She couldn't bring herself to repeat her mother's

cold words.

"She's too out there for me, and I just couldn't see wasting a whole night with someone I have nothing in common with."

"Sorry it went like that." He pulled her close wrapping his arms around her. "I'm glad you're here, with me."

She pressed her face against his shoulder trying to fight back the tears that were stinging their way out. She pulled away and plopped down on the edge of the bed embarrassed by the wet face print she left on his shoulder.

"There's a place I want to show you." He opened the window and waited for her to climb out. The thought of running again was a relief, so she was out the window and on the sidewalk before he finished closing up.

She was tight on his heels through the city. He stopped at a steep flight of stairs that led up to a glowing white building with towers and domes.

"Wow."

"It's closed so we have to find our own way in," he grinned.

Ada gave him a suspicious smile as they started up.

The building stood on the highest hill in Paris. It took several flights of stairs before they came to the base. They followed a fence to a dimly lit area, where a sturdy branch helped them to the other side. There wasn't a person in sight, but they kept in the shadows until they came to a large wooden door slightly ajar.

It opened to a small sanctuary empty of people.

Someone had to be in the vicinity because of a table full of flickering candles. Ada leaned her head back and gazed at the towering dome ceiling. When they heard voices echoing in a nearby hall, Daniel grabbed her hand and guided her in and out of door wells and up a spiral staircase. They stepped out into the open air of a circular covered balcony.

"This is so amazing," she said rushing up to a glassless arched window that framed Paris. It stretched in every direction like a blanket of twinkling lights. She watched the Eiffel Tower shimmer and sparkle against the darkness. France hadn't felt so exotic or foreign until that moment. Even the crisp smell of the night air carried something new.

She stared for a long time in silence at the busy cityscape, until he showed her to another area, where they dropped down onto a flat rooftop. The domes and tower pressed in around them framing the night sky. They lay back and watched the stars slowly start to fade.

"Do you have to go back now?"

"You didn't have to bring me here to make me want to stay." She rolled over on her side to face him. "No place has felt more like home." She leaned forward as Daniel ran his hand up her back and into her hair pulling her close and kissing her.

They talked on the rooftop until daylight. On their way out they passed a bewildered priest coming across the cobblestone toward the sanctuary.

"You can't be in here. We're closed," he said as they climbed the stone wall and disappeared over to the other side.

16

A month had passed since the night at the lab. Ada had been helping Daniel clean and stock the store until early afternoon and then running with the group until late. She still had her morning lessons with Uncle Henri who was happy with her progress and the fact that he was in shape again. Madame Jardin had finally returned to her apartment without any problems, and Ada had brought Daniel over to meet her.

Everything in Ada's life was going great except that Jessie still hadn't answered any of her emails. She had written and told her about finding Simone, but still no word. More than ever Ada realized that Jessie was the closest thing she had to family, and she didn't want to let that go. Not hearing from her made her think of Vancouver and the senator. She thought about flying back to search, but Professor Strathern was the only connection she had. It wasn't hard to find his email address at the university. He had already written back expressing his concern, but also reassuring her that Jessie was known for disappearing and then resurfacing.

Ada and Daniel were getting ready to meet Florien and Elaine to practice. Florien hadn't pushed for answers about what had happened on the rooftop of the lab between Ada and the guard, but he was suspicious. She felt she could trust them but the right time to talk hadn't come up.

They found an unused stretch of tunnel alongside the subway tracks to practice in. The goal was to get from one end of the tunnel to the other without touching the ground. Daniel was the first to make it, running along the wall and then launching back and forth between the wall and thick concrete columns that separated the platform they were on from the tracks below. Ada tried following Daniel's path, but barely made it a quarter of the way.

"You're getting stronger," Daniel said smiling.

They stood and watched Florien make his way down the tunnel doing flips and twists off of the wall and columns.

"Stunts like that look good but you lose efficiency," Daniel said just as Florien's foot slipped off the side of a column and he was flung to the tracks below. They jumped down to see if he was hurt.

"I think... I need the hospital," Florien said through clenched teeth as he rocked back and forth cradling his forearm.

"Let's see it," Daniel said. Florien carefully pulled his hand away. In the middle of his forearm the tip of a snapped bone protruded from a bloody tear in his skin.

"Oh shit, Florien!" Elaine gasped covering her mouth.

"Can I see it?"Ada said kneeling down in front of him. She gently laid her hands on his arm.

"Don't touch it!" Elaine yelled. "You could make it worse."

Within seconds Ada stepped back next to Daniel.

"I told you!" Florien said jumping to his feet and pointing to his perfectly smooth arm. "Didn't I tell you something was weird about her." He laughed bringing his healed arm right up to Elaine's face. "I knew she did something to me that day."

"No. This isn't real," Elaine said shaking her head back and forth. "You guys are messing with me."

"I wanted to explain, but I have to be careful."

"So you can just touch anyone and they're fixed?" Florien asked.

"Pretty much. I mean there's other stuff that goes on, but I do have to touch the person."

Elaine pulled up her pant leg revealing a deep black and blue bruise on her shin the size of a silver dollar.

"I did this on the stairs." She looked up at Ada. "So, if you touch it, it'll just go away?" As fast as Ada laid three fingers across the bruise it faded and was gone.

"That's fucking awesome!" Florien said punching at the air. "Let's go find Etienne and his gang and just beat the shit out of them and then she can fix us."

Daniel laughed and shook his head. "No one can find out."

Ada told them about her experiences with the senator and his men.

"Yeah, I bet they want you," Florien said with a serious expression. "You've saved me twice, thanks."

"That's why you followed us and wanted to learn Parkour in the first place, so they won't be able to catch you," Elaine said.

"Pretty much."

"Sorry I was such a jerk when we first met."

"It's cool," Ada smiled.

They left the subway and spent the rest of the night running the streets. Pushing herself and then healing made Ada stronger and faster. She could feel the changes in her body but most of all in her courage. The next time she met up with the senator things would be different.

As Uncle Henri prepared the front room for their training session Ada found an internet signal a few doors down from the store. She sat at the bottom of the porch pulling up her email. She had tried to convince Uncle Henri to let her have internet hooked up but he refused just as he refused TV. He told her that hard work and the newspaper were enough to keep people busy until they die. A little envelope appeared on the screen letting her know she had mail. She could hardly wait the seconds it took to download.

"Yes!" she said aloud startling a lady passing by.

It was from Jessie. Her heart fell a little when she saw only a short paragraph.

Dear Ada,

I'm sorry for not writing sooner. I've been busy at a hospital. It's wonderful news that you found Simone. I don't have the time to say everything I would like to, but I would love to see you. I have a lot I need to tell you. I will be at the Capilano Suspension Bridge in Vancouver in three days. I hope to see you there.

Love,

Jessie

"Wonderful?" Since when did Jessie think anything to do with Simone was wonderful, Ada mumbled to herself, re-reading the email several times. She closed her laptop and headed to the apartment to tell Daniel about the email.

"Have her come here," Daniel said. Uncle Henri nodded in agreement.

Ada knew Daniel didn't want her to leave, but she couldn't bring Jessie to Paris until she talked to her in person. It was too risky.

"I think it's better if I meet her and then maybe she'll come back with me." Ada smiled at Daniel, "I really want you to meet her."

Ada had three days to get to Vancouver. She bought a plane ticket to leave that evening. Daniel borrowed Uncle Henri's delivery van to drive her to the airport. There wasn't enough time to visit, so she had to say goodbye to Madame Jardin over the phone. Before they left, Uncle Henri gave her a long hug and made sure she understood that the third bedroom was hers.

The plane was already boarding when they arrived. She was usually happy when she left a place, but this was the first place she actually didn't want to leave.

Ada and Daniel hugged until a ticketing lady tapped her on the shoulder asking her if she was a passenger.

Daniel kissed her before she could pull away, "Please come back."

"I will. I promise," she said wanting to forget the whole trip and go with him instead, but her worries for Jessie pulled her away and up the boarding ramp toward an anxious stewardess motioning her forward. She took one last look back before boarding the plane to see Daniel still watching.

The plane ride was going to be long and depressing. If Ada wasn't thinking of Daniel running through the streets of Paris without her, she was thinking of what she would say to Jessie. The seats next to her were empty, so she had her choice of window or aisle seat.

In front of her, she overheard a French couple talking about taking their daughter to a clinic in Canada. Occasionally she caught a glimpse of a small hand reaching between the seats or pressed against the window.

When the stewardess brought food the little girl poked her head above the back of the chair trying to see what Ada had on her tray.

Sickness was around for a reason Ada told herself as she looked away from the child's sunken eyes and ghostly pale skin. She could spend every minute of the rest of her life healing strangers and she wouldn't even dent the suffering in the world, possibly only making it worse by overcrowding or healing cruel people.

Ada moved her untouched food onto the chair next to her, and breathed a sigh of relief when the little girl disappeared behind the seat. She could see what was going on with the girl's system, but knowing this didn't make her obligated to fix it. She leaned her head back and closed her eyes. The crackling sound of plastic caused her to sit up. The little girl was back, perched above the seat, with a bag of cookies in her outstretched hand. Ada shook her head no and stared out the window at the silver streaked blackness.

"Catherine quit bothering people." A lady's head now appeared above the middle seat, "I'm sorry if she's bothering you."

"She's not," Ada said standing to go to the bathroom.

Her face was a blur in the mirror that looked like the dull side of tin foil. She splashed her face with water and reminded herself that this wasn't her business. She took her seat again and pressed her forehead against the cold window.

"Catherine quit staring and sit straight."

Ada looked up to see a smiling face peering at her from between the seat and window. She couldn't help but laugh, so she held out her hand wiggling her fingers. The face was replaced by an out stretched hand. Ada grabbed it letting the warm energy flow into Catherine. Within seconds Catherine forced her other hand through the gap and pressed it into Ada's.

They stayed like that long after the healing was done. It was strange to feel the confusion change to calm. Ada thought it interesting how Catherine's immune system worked quickly to correct the problem while Madame Cornot's took more time and energy.

When the hands disappeared and the face returned, Ada saw that Catherine's dark sunken circles and ashen skin tone were gone. She reached in her backpack and pulled out her iPod. After all, if Catherine wouldn't have reached for her hand she wouldn't have got involved. She leaned her head back and started thinking about what she could say to convince Jessie to come back to France with her.

Catherine had managed to find her way back to the seat next to Ada. Her parents were so overwhelmed by the sudden change in her appearance and overflowing energy that when she climbed over the seat to sit next to Ada they smiled at her imploringly.

The rest of the trip was spent listening to music and watching Catherine color pictures.

BFF

In no time the pilot was announcing the landing. Ada tried to exit the plane quickly, but Catherine's parents managed to keep up all the way through customs. Ada had no luggage so she tried to veer away toward an exit.

"Is someone picking you up?" the mother asked smiling.

"Yep, someone's picking me up," Ada stopped and faced them.

Catherine ran up holding out both hands, so Ada kneeled down taking them.

"You're alright now Catherine. It's your mom and dad who need the reassurance," Ada whispered.

She stood quickly and nodded to the parents as she hurried off to find a shuttle bus. Taxis in this town were out of the question. On the way out the door she glanced over her shoulder to find Catherine and her parents still watching.

17

By the time the shuttle dropped Ada off at the hotel and she ate dinner, it was late afternoon. She was staying in the ivy covered hotel across from the beach. It was the only place that came to mind when the shuttle driver asked where she was staying.

She spent the rest of the night listening to music and surfing the internet. Jessie hadn't said an exact time to meet and she wasn't answering emails again, so Ada decided to be at the park right when it opened.

She caught the same bus as before, and watched the same landscape blur by. This time spattered with fall colors of orange and brown.

The park was open, but she had to squeeze past a group of people arguing in front of the gates. No one was in sight at the entrance counter so she left the money next to the register. It seemed she had the park to herself. Her footsteps were light but they crackled through the twigs and leaves breaking the silence.

Ada sat down on the bench she and Jessie had talked on before, and looked out at the empty bridge. It wasn't long before she heard footsteps coming up the path. She stood to meet Jessie halfway but stopped dead in her tracks. Less than fifteen feet in front of her stood the senator. She heard more footsteps and rustling from the bushes around her. She was surrounded.

Before the senator could say a word, she shot out onto the suspension bridge only to find a man waiting at the other side.

"Hold on now Ada, no one is going to hurt you," the senator said walking awkwardly onto the bridge, each hand tensely grasping at the chain link guard rail.

"Where's Jessie?" Ada yelled walking further toward the middle of the bridge. She looked from side to side realizing she was being cornered.

"She's waiting for you at my villa. That's the only reason we're here, so we can take you to Jessie." He kept moving slowly toward her as two more men came behind him.

"You're lying!" she yelled as she backed further out onto the bridge, "I can smell that you're sick."

The senator winced and then nodded to the man coming across the bridge from the other side.

"Jessie would have healed you if she was happily waiting for me at your villa."

"Certain names alert us; Simone Larue is one of them. We started intercepting your emails over a month ago. It didn't take long to figure out what we needed to say to get you to meet us." He laughed at her annoyance.

The man on the other side was moving in fast.

"Don't come any closer or I swear to God I'll jump!" she yelled flinging one of her legs over the side of the guardrail, causing the bridge to rock back and forth.

Both men came to a startled halt. The senator braced himself frantically against the swaying bridge. The bottom of the canyon had a flowing river, but up this high, it looked like a withered brown stream. She thought that all of the jumps across rooftops had ended her fear of heights, but the old dizzy feeling and watering mouth was overtaking her.

"Ada," the senator gasped, "the last thing I want is for you to kill yourself."

"I know exactly what you want, a personal slave," she interrupted.

"Not at all, I will protect you Ada," he said with a pleading look. "There are numerous agencies and individuals hunting down healers but with me you would be safe and living in luxury." He took a small step toward her.

"Freedom is the only luxury I want."

Looking down was no longer an option. Her spinning head was making her stomach sick. The drop to the bottom of the ravine seemed a hundred times higher than any building she had jumped or even fallen from.

"Freedom is an illusion. You're in hiding because you're hunted. Even those you think you can trust believe a gift like yours belongs to humanity as a whole, and your freedom is a necessary sacrifice. Let me help you." The senator exchanged a look with the man on the other side who then took a step forward.

It was at that moment Ada realized the bottom of the ravine was her only way out. The senator would call her bluff and rush forward. Her true freedom was her will to survive. That's how it would be from now on. A cool breeze brushed the hair from her face. This was either the end of her fear of heights or the limit of her healing ability, whichever one it didn't matter. They were both only obstacles.

She turned to the senator with a smile, wiping the smug look from his face.

"Grab her!" he screamed charging feebly toward her.

But it was too late; she'd already let go. She made sure to push off hard sending the bridge lurching back and forth. Her stomach felt like it was pushing up through her throat, but all her focus was on healing her body.

Once the treetops started to densely frame the blue sky she knew the ground was close. The healing energy made her bones and skin seem on fire. She felt like a meteor streaking toward impact.

The pain shattered through her body, but it was quickly neutralized, and her mind stayed perfectly clear. When she finally stopped bouncing and lay still against the cold wet rocks, water swooshed into her ear forcing her to sit up and look around. She had landed on the edge of the river. During the fall or on impact, she couldn't be sure, her backpack had been pulled off.

All of its contents lay scattered around her, including multiple pieces of her laptop.

She stood to see the senator. He was looking down at her with several of his men on each side. She couldn't make out the expression on his face, but from his body language she could see he was more shocked than defeated. There was no time to gloat. She quickly gathered up her things and started walking along the river bank.

Before heading into the woods she took one last look back. The senator was still standing on the bridge watching her, but this time he was alone. She broke into a run.

All she had to do was get back to the streets. There, they would never catch her.

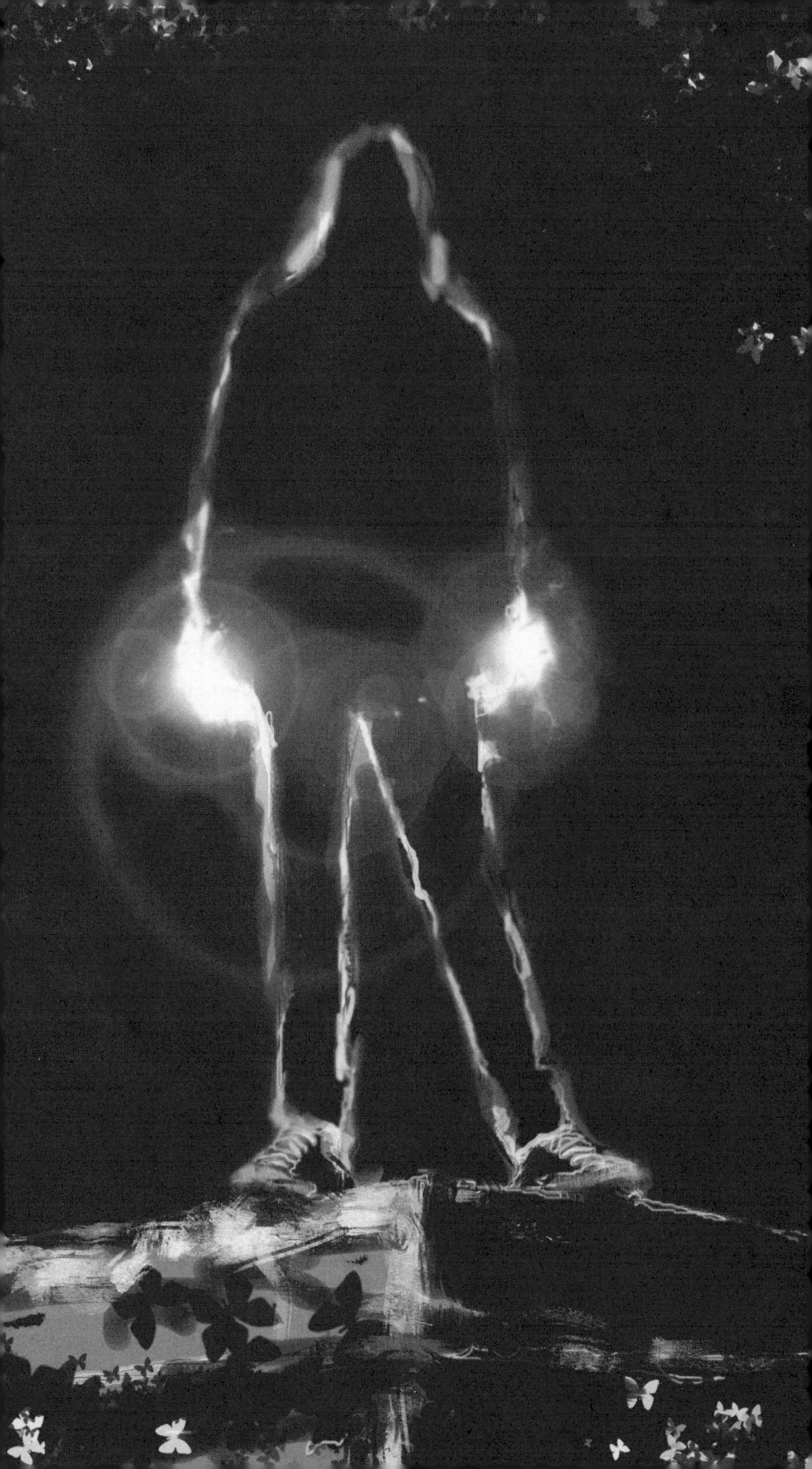

Questions to Consider

1. If you had the power to heal, do you feel it would be your duty to help as many people as you can? Jessie believes a healer should heal everyone they can. Ada believes careful thought and personal choice should be what direct a healer. What do you think?
2. Jessie says that for the first time she understands why some things should be forced in order to help humanity as a whole. Should the betterment of humanity be considered more important than the rights of an individual?
3. When Ada hit the boy in the head with a bat she was sent away. Should she have handled this situation differently? If so, how?
4. Ada tells Professor Strathern that sickness is around for a reason and that she's not interested in helping him turn the world into standing room only. Would the world become standing room only if sickness and injury were gone?
5. Professor Strathern believes that if humanity was free of sickness people would follow and accept laws on population control. Ada doesn't believe effective laws could be put in place by politicians like Senator Grimes. What do you think?
6. Ada makes the comment, "Downtown was safe to disappear in during the day, but deadly, or worse at night." How can a location be safe during the day and unsafe at night? Does this idea apply to all cities? What does this say about a community and its priorities?
7. How much is the mind involved in the healing process? Does today's health care system support and encourage this inner practice?
8. What did Madame Cornot mean when she said the nurses and doctors only see her as cancer?
9. Why does strong will represent freedom to Ada? What has to go hand in hand with a strong will to make it positive or beneficial? What do you believe true freedom is?

We would love to hear your answers to the questions above. Go to www.AdasLegend.com to post them and interact with others about them.

R.A. McDonald lives in the
Pacific Northwest with her family.

THE LEGEND CONTINUES